D1503284

DISCARD

Wyoming Trail

**Center Point
Large Print**

**This Large Print Book carries the
Seal of Approval of N.A.V.H.**

Wyoming Trail

WALKER A. TOMPKINS

CENTER POINT PUBLISHING
THORNDIKE, MAINE

This Center Point Large Print edition
is published in the year 2011 by arrangement with
Golden West Literary Agency.

First published in the US by Pheonix Press.
First published in the UK by Hutchinson.

The text of this Large Print edition is unabridged.
In other aspects, this book may vary
from the original edition.
Printed in the United States of America
on permanent paper.
Set in 16-point Times New Roman type.

ISBN: 978-1-61173-215-3

Library of Congress Cataloging-in-Publication Data

Tompkins, Walker A.
Wyoming trail / Walker A. Tompkins.
p. cm.
ISBN 978-1-61173-215-3 (library binding : alk. paper)
1. Wyoming—Fiction. 2. Large type books. I. Title.
PS3539.O3897W96 2011
813'.52—dc22

2011023022

TO

GRACE L. SPEAR

CONTENTS

Wyoming Trail

I
ADIOS TO ELBOWROOM

STUNNED by surprise, Quent Preston and his white-bearded father drew rein on the ridge crest, and stared in mute astonishment at the scene of confusion around Wagonwheel Springs.

So unexpectedly had the Texans come upon the dusty bedlam on the flat below that the shock left them speechless. Only yesterday, it seemed, Wagonwheel Springs had been a somnolent waterhole known only to wild life and an occasional Indian or frontiersman.

Now the waterhole had become the nucleus of a teeming mushroom city. Two streets threaded their way from the springs. Some enterprising persons had already thrown a peeled-pole fence about the precious water supply and its shading cottonwood trees.

With incredulous eyes, the Prestons stared down the slope at the false-fronted shacks which were being erected along the east-west street. Gaudy signs were readable from the hilltop: "Red Tent Saloon"; "Slidge & Spike Dance Hall"; "U. P. Poker Palace"; "End of Track Hotel."

Unfamiliar sounds wafted up to the Texans who had ridden out of the Sioux Bonnet mountain country—noise utterly foreign to the lonely Wyoming terrain. The racketing of hammers and saws; the metallic discord of sledges hitting steel spikes; the undertone of shouting men, the clang of a remote bell, braying mules, the hiss of escaping steam.

The only warning they had had of something unusual was when the familiar pine forest had suddenly given way to a naked hilltop stubbled with heaps of brush and stumps from which newly-hewn chips were slowly browning under the sun.

But the town below—Quent Preston passed a rope-scarred hand across his eyes, as if to erase the ugliness of the sprawling acres of tents and shacks which spoiled the landscape. Men bustled like ants amid those canvas roofs, weltering masses of bewhiskered, roughly dressed men toiling in a pandemonium of activity without visible unity of purpose.

"What in hell is goin' on down there?" The cowboy voiced the question hoarsely, as if unable to comprehend the meaning of what he saw. Yet he knew the truth, before Panhandle Preston straightened his ramrod spine and drawled huskily:

"It's that Union Pacific Railroad they was telling us about at Fort Laramie last fall. It's caught up with us."

As if to corroborate the oldster's words, there

came from somewhere below the long, deep blast of a locomotive whistle. Only then did Quent Preston realize the significance of the logged-off timber about them. A forest had been leveled for railroad ties and stacked like cordwood on the flats below in unbroken ricks a quarter of a mile in length.

Quent Preston's sun-wizened countenance hardened perceptibly as he adjusted his Stetson brim against slanting sun rays. A lean, whippy man of thirty, he sensed the unvoiced grief in his father's voice; experienced the same tug of resignation in the depths of his own being—a pang of spirit such as the Indian knew when the white man trespassed his hunting grounds.

"It's *adios* to elbowroom for us, I reckon." Quent's drawl held the same restraint that had marked his father's. "I never thought a railroad would have ever tromped our heels out here."

His gaze swiveled under knotted brows, in an effort to avoid the turmoil of the construction camp below. He found scant solace in the purple vista of the Wyoming hills to eastward.

The vanishing V of the railroad cleft the horizon there. It was a tangible symbol linking this frontier to civilization. And civilization was oppressive to these elemental cowmen.

"Anyhow, the waterhole is still down there," grunted Panhandle Preston, gathering up his reins. "That's what we came here for. Might as

13

well water our horses and then head for the ranch."

They rolled their spurs reluctantly, as if steeling themselves against an ordeal.

No one in the bustling throngs paid any attention to the horsemen who picked their way down the stump-dotted slope toward the raucous traffic of the main street. The Prestons were alien to this Wyoming scene, with their bat-wing chaps that still bore the scuffs of Texas mesquite and sage. Yet they fitted into the wild landscape. Their rugged exteriors and taciturn bearing marked them as men of a tough breed, who had come to this uncurried outland and had conquered it by sheer sweat and will and brawn.

Their Stetsons were higher of crown and wider of brim sweep than the boom-camp residents'. Their shirts were of pliable buckskin with fringed sleeves and buffalo-horn buttons.

Neither of the Prestons wore sidearms—a factor that was sharply at variance with the rough, hard men about them. Along the U. P. trail, revolvers were kept clear for action, and this new town would undoubtedly know the bloodshed and violence that had marked Kearney and Medicine Hat and Cheyenne and other camps.

Both Prestons carried Winchester carbines in their saddle boots, however. The rifles showed the signs of rough and frequent usage, as did their saddles and high-heeled boots.

Knots of muscle gritted in Quent Preston's jaws as they tooled their ponies hurriedly out of mid-street to avoid being run down by a troop of blue-uniformed cavalry that came galloping in massed formation out of the side street, on their way to barracks.

The sight of glittering sabers and cartridge bandoliers told their own story to Quent Preston. The United States Army was the sole protection the railroad crews had against the Sioux, who were on the warpath against the encroaching whites.

Hints of the red man's dogged resistance had reached the Prestons from the lips of the occasional trappers and prospectors who had visited their lonely ranch back in Tomahawk Pass.

"Men," grunted Panhandle, "can turn God's country into hell—"

The younger Preston nodded assent. His head whirled from the noise and chaos behind the smoking mantle of alkali dust. Hoofs thudded and men yelled. A rock-eyed woman with painted lips screamed an obscene epithet as her billowing skirts were sprayed with gravel by Quent's horse in passing.

He shuddered. A woman's oath—it typified the evil of this city of tents and clapboard which had come like a cancerous growth to defile the land.

"Waal—if it ain't the Prestons! Come to pay our meetropolis a visit, hey?"

The Texans halted alongside the fence which

surrounded the waterhole, searching the stream of buffeting humanity to trace the ownership of the sneering, but familiar, voice.

Then they spotted the chunky, barrel-chested figure of Cy Trollen, clad in Levis and straw hat and packing double six-guns at his hips, hunkered like a foul vulture on the top rail of the gate entering Wagonwheel Springs.

Only once before had the Prestons met Cy Trollen, their only American neighbor in this section of Wyoming. That had been one day the previous fall, when Quent had caught Trollen in the act of blotting the brand on a Lone Star critter that had strayed from the herd of longhorns the Prestons were hazing over to their Tomahawk Pass range.

Trollen's nose had not mended well after its encounter with Quent's fist on that occasion. It increased the ugliness of an already ugly face, and brought a flush of recollection to the cowboy now, as he piled hands on saddlehorn.

"Howdy, Trollen." Quent avoided the rustler's leer as he surveyed the springs behind the fence. A man and a girl were dismounting under the cottonwoods there, to fill their canteens.

"If that's a gate you're settin' on," called Panhandle, "oblige us by openin' it, Trollen. Our bronc ain't watered since we left the Beavertail. We were huntin' water when we stumbled across this damn beehive you call a meetropolis."

16

Trollen clambered down off the gate and unbarred it. The Prestons dismounted and stretched catlike to unkink saddle-weary muscles. Out of saddle, their unusual height became apparent for the first time—six feet four of lean brawn, father and son, without benefit of steeple-peaked hats.

"Water for your stock and canteens will set you back a dollar a head," Trollen informed them, holding out a big palm as Preston started to lead his buckskin into the inclosure. "I got the waterhole concession in this town."

Preston halted, frowning as if he had not heard Trollen aright.

"Wagonwheel Springs is on public land," he said with a mirthless smile. "Stock been watering free here before you hit this country, Trollen, and they'll keep on doin' it."

"Wake up!" Trollen's voice, thickened by the alcohol which revolted Quent's nostrils, took on a note of menace as Trollen dropped a hairy fist to the butt of a six-gun. "You lookin' for trouble? Things is different, now that Wagonwheel is a hell-raisin' railroad town. You'll ante up, by God, or you don't water up!"

Quent Preston pushed forward, his voice deceptively calm:

"Move aside, Trollen. We been a-waterin' here long before you saw Wagonwheel. We—"

Trollen's hand lifted from holster to jab the

front sight of a heavy .45 Colt into Quent's side.

"You've overplayed your hand once too often, Preston!" snarled the waterhole keeper furiously, cocking the gun. "You and me got a score to settle anyhow, and now's as good a time as—"

Quent Preston's right hand released the bit ring of his saddle pony and lashed upward in a short uppercut which landed against Trollen's jaw with crunching impact.

Slammed sprawling before he could jerk his trigger finger, the ruffian struck the gatepost with jarring force.

For an instant Trollen leaned against the gatepost, his eyes glazing. Then his boots slid on the hoof-trampled soil and he thudded heavily to the ground.

A grayish look wiped the congested color from Trollen's brutal face. Blood gushed unexpectedly from the back of his head, as he toppled sidewise and lay twitching in the dust.

Blood dripped, likewise, from the glistening point of a heavy nail which protruded from the pine gatepost. Three inches of sharp iron projecting from the wood, where a corral bar had been spiked against the gatepost.

Quent squatted down by Trollen's limp form, examining the gory wound at the base of the man's skull. Then he looked up at Panhandle and said dispassionately:

"Trollen's dead."

II

END-OF-TRACK JUSTICE

WAGONWHEEL boasted only one building which could lay claim to an outward semblance of permanence or solidity. That was the frame structure used as the field headquarters of the Union Pacific. It was transported in sections each time it was moved ahead to end-of-track, and from its office was handled the complicated business of the railroad. On rare intervals it was visited by General Dodge, chief engineer in charge of the mighty cross-country enterprise, on his inspection tours.

It was significant that at each new townsite the U. P. office was always flanked by a crude shack bearing the painted legend:

BAYARD'S LAND OFFICE
Ellis Bayard, Attorney
RIGHT-OF-WAY CLAIMS
ARE OUR SPECIALTY

Bayard was a pompous, flashily dressed individual with an onion-bald skull, his moonlike face pink-shaven except for the brown muttonchops which furred his jowls.

This morning he was in the act of tacking a big

railroad map on the wall above his desk, when someone rapped a familiar tattoo on his front door.

"Come in, Delivan."

The door opened to admit a tall, powerfully built man with a swarthy, handsome face. His excellently tailored clothing and polished demeanor were oddly out of place in the wild environment of a Western construction camp.

"Well—this is the last time my office will be torn down and set up, I guess," greeted Bayard, as his visitor removed a high beaver hat and ran fingers through a crop of raven-black hair. "Three hundred more miles, and the Union Pacific will be finished."

Boone Delivan glanced about the room to make sure he had no listener, and said in a controlled voice that hinted inner excitement:

"It's closer to being finished than you know, Bayard. My scouts, Averill and DePerren, got back from the Sioux Bonnets last night. Their report tied in with confidential information I've picked up on my own. Wait till you hear—"

Delivan paused as the lawyer poured him a glass of bourbon from a bottle in his desk.

A man of mystery around end-of-track was Boone Delivan. He had dropped no hint of his past even to Bayard, his closest associate. But his courtly manners and refined language bespoke a genteel background that made his presence at end-of-track a puzzle to all who met him.

Delivan's cravat pin and diamond finger ring were modest and in perfect taste—otherwise Delivan would have suggested a professional gambler, a type common to the riffraff which followed the westward-crawling Union Pacific, parasites preying on the vast armies of workmen, engineers and soldiers.

This classification would have only been partially correct in Delivan's case, however. He was, in truth, a gambler. But he played for vastly higher stakes than did the tinhorn card-sharps who frequented the main street's garish halls of chance.

No spinner of roulette wheel or dealer of poker hands was Boone Delivan. His weapons were brains and a suave personality; his opponents the men who owned land in the pathway of the history-making Union Pacific; his game was the profitable and often dangerous one of acquiring right of way by devious methods, and reselling it to the railroad at his own price.

As a private speculator, Boone Delivan had become a familiar, if unexplainable, figure in all the end-of-track camps that had flowered and died along the railroad west of Omaha.

"You were saying—" prompted Ellis Bayard, after Delivan had downed his whiskey and was snipping the end of a Cuban cheroot.

21

"What I am going to tell you is strictly confidential, of course," cautioned Delivan. "You know how the surveyors had given up the idea of crossing the Sioux Bonnet mountains, because of all the tunneling and trestle work involved?"

"Yes," answered the lawyer. "They're swinging around the south end of the range and then north again into Utah."

Delivan returned his cheroot to his teeth and fumbled in a flowered waistcoat for a match.

"That's where you are mistaken, Bayard. Some radical changes are going to be made in the U. P. survey from here on west. Even General Dodge is unaware of it as yet, but my information comes direct from a reliable source. The railroad will go through Tomahawk Pass."

Bayard gulped with surprise. "But the engineers rejected Tomahawk Pass," he protested. "The grade would be too steep—it would cost more to build than the longer route to the south—"

Delivan paused, lighted match at cheroot's tip.

"No. The railroad will go through the Pass," he repeated confidently. "And it happens that Tomahawk Pass is owned from rimrock to rimrock by a pair of cattlemen named Preston. My men found out as much for me. It's up to me to contact those Pres—"

A frenzied knocking at the door made Delivan whirl about. Before Bayard could call out, the door slammed open to reveal a cinnamon-bearded man whose rolled-up sleeves and grimy apron branded him as a bartender in one of the camp saloons.

"Delivan—there's a lynching party brewing up the street!" cried the saloon man. "A cowboy murdered the feller who fenced the waterhole, and Lige Morton, the marshal, has arrested him. The crowd's hollerin' for hang rope, and Morton says it's all right!"

Boone Delivan lit another match with an annoyed gesture.

"Don't bother me with boom-camp brawls, DePerren!" snapped the speculator impatiently. "I'm not interested in—"

"But the cowboy they're going to string up is one of those Preston hombres who own that ranch up in Tomahawk Pass!" cut in DePerren. "His father's with him. The same fellers me and Bob Averill saw up in the mountains a week ago—"

"The hell you say!"

Boone Delivan dropped his cigar and snatched up his beaver top hat. Without a backward look at Ellis Bayard, the speculator rushed out onto the street, accompanied by DePerren.

"We can't let Morton go through with this lynching!" cried Delivan, striding out onto a street where everyone had dropped his work and was running in the general direction of Wagonwheel Springs. "Get Averill and Clancy and back my play if the going gets rough, see?"

Delivan broke into a run as he caught sight of the throng which was milling about the waterhole fence. Dust blurred the scene, but Delivan recognized the town marshal, Lige Morton, in the act of flinging a rope over the low-hanging limb of one of the waterhole cottonwoods.

Lynch fever was in the air. The roar of the mob was already like the soul-chilling cry of a wolf pack. Lynchings were commonplace as shootings and knifings in the lawless U. P. camps. They were a safety valve that tapped the seething unrest of the tough citizenry. And Lige Morton catered to the mob's whims.

Boone Delivan reached the outskirts of the mob, a grim figure in black frock coat and boots polished to a high gloss. He commenced seizing men by arms and shoulders, flinging them roughly aside as he fought nearer the center of the maelstrom.

Uniformed soldiers and husky rail-layers; stocky Irish spikers and yellow Chinese laundrymen; pasty-complexioned saloon swampers and grimy repairmen from the U. P. repair shops—all were blended in a vortex of yelling, struggling humanity through which Boone Delivan fought and elbowed and cursed his way.

His eardrums throbbed to the onslaught of sound, shrill calls of Cain so common to hanging bees:

"Lynch the damned skunk!" "It was cold-blooded murder!" "Send the old-timer to hell along with his whelp!" "Show those bowlaiged cowpokes they're in a town tougher than they are!"

Sweat and churning alkali dust had made a mask over Delivan's face by the time he had clawed his way to the waterhole fence. He clambered over the rails and dropped into the inclosure, breathing heavily, his heart pounding with exertion. But he was not too late.

Both of the Prestons had their arms tied behind their backs and were in the custody of burly U. P. graders. Lige Morton, the cadaverous "city marshal" who wore the only law badge in camp and was careful not to impose his authority too openly, was busy adjusting the rolled loop of a hangman's knot about the younger cowman's neck.

Quent Preston's eyes were blackened and threads of blood leaked from bruised nostrils. His buckskin shirt was tattered and his knuckles were raw, signs of the resistance he had put up before the mob had overcome him by sheer force of numbers.

Behind Quent, Panhandle stood panting heavily, white hair streaming to his shoulders, his scalp oozing blood from a welt caused by a clubbing gun butt. Behind them their horses waited, nostrils flaring in alarm.

There was no mistaking the relationship of the

two: both had the same bone structure in brow and jaw, the same towering height, the same fearless blue gaze with a bearing of dignity and contempt for the roiling bedlam around them.

Boone Delivan strode around the muddy pool, hundreds of eyes following his tall, striking figure as he walked up to Lige Morton and seized the marshal by a bony shoulder.

"Keep out of this, Delivan!" "Get to hell away, Boone—"

The crowd roared with fresh venom, sensing that Delivan had come to intercede in favor of the intended lynch victims. Guns bellowed volleys of lead skyward; men cupped hands to mouths and screamed through the fence bars for Delivan to stand back and let Lige Morton get on with the hanging.

"What's the idea, Boone?" demanded the marshal, his breath coming in gusts as he stared up at the speculator. "You're interrupting justice here!"

"What's the charge against these strangers?" snapped Delivan, his black eyes flickering over Quent Preston. "I'm sick of seeing men die without their killers knowing what they did to deserve punishment! This crowd's just after excitement—"

Before Morton could overcome his surprise and grope for a reply, Quent Preston's low voice arrested Delivan's attention:

"You better not mix up in this, amigo—but thanks. That crowd's ugly and we're outnumbered. No use you losing your life—"

Delivan moved closer to the Prestons, oblivious to the ear-numbing din of the angry mob, which was crowding against the waterhole fence and threatening to smash it down.

"What happened here?" Delivan asked Quent.

"An accident!" shrilled Panhandle Preston, yelling across Quent's shoulder. "My son bashed Trollen's jaw to keep from bein' cut down by a bullet. Neither one of us was heeled. Trollen died when his noggin hit a spike. Then we were jumped by these street hoodlums and beat up, and this tin-star hollered for a rope!"

Boone Delivan turned to Lige Morton and before the lynchthirsty marshal was aware of the speculator's intentions, Delivan had jerked both of Morton's Colt .45s from their holsters and was earing the hammers back to full cock.

"You better not stick your horns into this, Delivan!" snarled the marshal. "Them people out there want to see these hombres stretch rope, and you ain't stoppin' 'em!"

Delivan's voice rasped from the corner of his mouth, his guns leveled at the marshal's body:

"Tell your men to untie their arms and take that noose off Preston's neck. Tell 'em that, Morton!"

Impelled by the authority in Delivan's command, the marshal sputtered, turned alternately red and sickly white, and then croaked out an order. The two Prestons found their wrists untied, and the burly railroad laborers removed the hangknot from Quent's throat.

Glancing over his shoulder, Boone Delivan rasped out:

"Bring your horses and follow me. Don't try to mount, or some rowdy on the far edge of the crowd might shoot. Come on!"

Guns jutting forth from either hip, Boone Delivan stalked toward the open gateway of the fence, past the limp corpse of Cy Trollen which sprawled where he had fallen.

The shrill death-calls of the street mob rose to a deafening crescendo. A rock whistled through the air, striking Delivan on the shoulder and making him go white with pain. Someone closer at hand hurled a handful of gravel at Panhandle's horse, causing the nervous mustang to rear and buck savagely before the white-haired oldster got it under control.

Undaunted, Delivan marched grimly through the gate, his unwavering guns making an aisle form in the closely packed throng in front of him.

Then, from somewhere over to the left, a six-gun started thundering. Quent Preston gasped as a slug creased the flesh over one shoulder, and a warm gush of blood stained his buckskins. Yet he kept on, following Boone Delivan straight toward hell—

III

DELIVAN'S OFFER

THE speculator swung his right hand across his body and threw down a Colt .45 in a short, chopping motion. Flame spat from the bore of the gun, and over by the fence corner a blacksmith with a smoking army pistol screamed with agony and clutched a bullet-smashed forearm.

The exchange of shots silenced the crowd, froze them into a rigid wall of hate.

"I'm only creased," gritted Quent, falling into step beside Delivan. "Keep moving."

Shoulders slightly hunched, black eyes swiveling from left to right, Boone Delivan strode straight into the crowd, watching men fling themselves aside in panic before his grim advance, cowed by his rock-hard face as well as by the twin guns.

On either side of Delivan strode the Texans, relief blending with a fierce challenge in their eyes as they trailed their horses through the narrow corridor that divided the hate-maddened crowd.

Neither cowman showed outward sign that he knew the peril of this gantlet they were running. Yet they heard the disgruntled throng closing in the gap behind them, fingering gun triggers and clutching knife hilts in a fever of indecision.

It was a critical moment—the most crucial in Boone Delivan's life, as well as in the lives of the men he was rescuing. Delivan was staking everything on his ability to judge the temper of the mob he defied.

Met singly, not one of this ugly-tempered rabble would have the guts or the spine to oppose him. But, as units in a mob, the factor of hysteria had to be reckoned with. A single hostile move from an individual—say a frenzied weakling made bold by whiskey—would start a fatal attack in which many bystanders might die.

Quent and Panhandle, marching at Delivan's either elbow, summed up the facts to the same total. Quent's neck still smarted from the hangman's chafing noose; his bullet-burned shoulder was numb and wet. Panhandle lurched as he walked, his aged body racked by the bruises and cuts administered by the mob's initial attack.

Admiration gleamed in Quent Preston's stony gaze—admiration and gratitude for the icy, unwavering courage of the man who was stalking deliberately down the street, shuttling eyes wilting the men that met their ruthless scrutiny.

But disaster lay ahead. The outer ranks of the mob began to block up before them, sullen men beginning to balk, refusing to give ground. At this moment, a hoarse yell rang out in the desperate hush:

"Let's get that damned gutless marshal and make Lige Morton tell how come he surrenders prisoners thataway! *He's* the man we ought to be rowelin'!"

The tension broke. In that moment, Delivan had won. The mob caught up the cry, turning their attention to Lige Morton, who was already cowering in retreat, losing himself in the jam.

Boone Delivan's lips flickered in an imperceptible grin as he led the Prestons out of the crowd into the vacant street. He knew the owner of that bawling voice had stemmed the tide of peril that would have engulfed them in another few seconds.

That voice had belonged to DePerren, his own henchman. That timely yell had swerved the avalanche of wrath over to Lige Morton. It had been worth a dozen gunmen backing Delivan's play with force.

They did not halt until Delivan reached Bayard's land office, a block away. There he slowly pocketed Morton's guns, and turned to face the men he had snatched from the jaws of doom.

"I . . . I've seen some brave men in my time, amigo," whispered Panhandle Preston, grasping Delivan's hand fervently. "But you top the list. It took guts to buffalo a mob as boogery as that one back there, Mr. . . . Mr.—"

"Delivan."

The speculator shook hands with Quent, wiping dust and sweat from his face with his other hand.

"We owe you our hides, Delivan," said Quent Preston, fingering his bullet-scratched shoulder gingerly. "We won't soon forget it. Our name's Preston. This is my father."

Delivan swatted dust from his lapels and sleeves, his eyes narrowing in concern at the bloodstain on Quent's buckskin shirt.

"You hit bad, Preston?"

"Only a scratch. Doesn't hurt as much as the beatin' that cowardly outfit give us over by the spring."

Delivan stared down the street, and grinned. The lynch mob was already broken up, Morton having disappeared in the nick of time. There was a general exodus toward saloon bars and poker dens, and an almost carnival spirit filled the atmosphere.

"You men had better get out of camp as soon as possible," advised Delivan. "Some drunk might try to put a bullet through you. Life is cheap here—as the unmarked graves back along the Union Pacific tracks can testify."

Quent turned to his saddle, lifted a stirrup leather and cinched up a latigo strap. He grinned wryly and said:

"Anyhow, I noticed our broncs watered up at the springs while that mob was manhandlin' us. We're ready to ride, all right."

At that moment, Ellis Bayard's portly bulk appeared in the doorway of his office, watching as the Texans mounted.

"Where you from, strangers?" asked the lawyer impersonally. "Those chaps and spurs don't look like you work for the U. P."

"We don't savvy this iron horse business," grinned the cowboy. "No—me and dad own the Lone Star Ranch, up in the Sioux Bonnet country. In Tomahawk Pass."

"It's too bad," remarked Ellis Bayard, with a quick look at Boone Delivan, "that the railroad won't go through your pass. You could have made a mint of money on right of way sales if the surveyors hadn't condemned Tomahawk Pass."

Panhandle Preston stuffed some cut plug in his mouth and snorted. "We don't want any of the U. P.'s dinero. We're damned glad the railroad *can't* go through the pass."

Boone Delivan stepped forward, as if taking a sudden interest in the trend of the conversation.

"You say you own a cattle ranch?" he asked Quent. "How good a ranch? Plenty of grass and water?"

"Yeah. Why you askin', Mr. Delivan?"

Delivan waited until he had lighted up a cheroot. His voice sounded casual as he said:

"Oh, I happen to be a cattleman myself. From Omaha. Fact is, the reason I'm here is because I came out on the train to look for cattle range here

33

in Wyoming. I might be interested in buying your Tomahawk Pass ranch, if you care to sell. The price doesn't matter."

Quent looked down at the speculator and shook his head.

"Delivan, after what you just done for us, we'd be powerful glad to oblige you. But the Lone Star ain't for sale at any price, and never will be. Dad and I aim to live and die there. And I reckon the quicker we start for home, the better."

"No matter," shrugged Delivan, his poker face impassive. "Good-by—and good luck, both of you."

Wheeling their mustangs, the Texans waved in farewell and galloped out of town, heading for the Sioux Bonnet range which saw-toothed the skyline fifty miles away toward Utah.

IV

THE LAST BARRIER

BOONE DELIVAN stared absently into space, watching the Prestons dwindle into specks in the distance. His reverie was broken by the arrival of a horse and rider, and he looked up to see a girl drawing rein beside him, her wide and troubled eyes meeting his own. Instantly Delivan's manner changed.

"Why, Helen!" he exclaimed, removing his top hat and bowing slightly in the instinctive gentlemanly gesture he had practiced here amid the uncouth surroundings of the construction camp. "I supposed you and Major Gorine would be well on your way out to the survey camp by this time!"

Helen Gorine pointed behind her, to where a tall rider with white goatee and the plaid shirt, high-laced boots and military breeches of a civil engineer was riding up with a laden pack mule trailing by a hackamore.

"We were delayed getting my pony shod," she explained. "Boone, we happened to be filling our canteens at the springs when . . . when that awful thing happened. I want you to know we thought it was a brave thing for you to do, risking your life in behalf of those strangers just now. That

35

bloodthirsty mob—I shudder to think what they might have done to you for interfering."

Delivan laughed at her concern. Helen was the daughter of the Union Pacific's chief surveyor, Major John Gorine; but her visits to the end-of-track camps were seldom. Her place was always beside her father, cooking for the survey crew which kept its pace some fifty miles in advance of the roadbed and bridge crews.

"We saw the whole thing, Delivan," spoke up Major Gorine, spurring alongside his daughter's stirrup. "The cowboy struck in self-defense—the killing was purely accidental. I was starting over to put in a word for the cowboy myself, when I saw you arrive."

Delivan laughed again, and replaced his beaver hat.

"Well, I'll be riding out to your camp tomorrow, Helen," he said.

After the Gorines had loped off down the street in the same direction the Prestons had taken, Delivan turned about to see his bartender henchman, Linn DePerren, walking up. A broad grin was under DePerren's cinnamon whiskers.

Abruptly, Delivan's manner hardened.

"Good work back there, DePerren," he said shortly. "Got me out of a tough situation. Come on inside Bayard's place. We have plans to make."

The heavy-paunched lawyer moved aside to

36

admit the two men, and closed the door to shut out the increasing traffic noise.

"Delivan, I'll be damned if I can figure you out sometimes," said Bayard. "You risked your life to save those Prestons. And all it netted you was the admiration of a . . . a trollop who dresses like a man. It isn't like you, Delivan—to take risks like that."

Delivan shot the lawyer a queer glance. He turned to the big wall map of Wyoming and Utah which Bayard had tacked up, and peered closely at the red line which wriggled across the map, indicating the trackage already laid by the Union Pacific. The red mark ended fifty miles east of the rugged Sioux Bonnets, a mighty barrier between end-of-track and the terminal in Utah.

"I never run risks—unless I feel the stakes justify it," said Delivan musingly. "As for that trollop who dresses like a man—do you know who she is?"

Bayard grunted negatively.

"She happens to be Helen Gorine, daughter of the U. P.'s ace surveyor. From her I learned about Major Gorine's survey crew running the line through Tomahawk Pass. Her father believes he can divert Beavertail River from its bed, set a compound curve by intersections along the north wall—and remain under the maximum allowable grade of ninety feet to the mile."

37

Bayard's fat-creased jaw sagged with amazement at this news.

"When Gorine turns in his report, the U. P. will cut the distance to Ogden by half," Delivan continued. "A few more months of construction—and the Irish paddies of the Union Pacific will be meeting the Chinese coolies who are building the Central Pacific out of California—and America will be spanned by rail."

Bayard seated himself at his desk and poured a drink.

"You win, so far," admitted the lawyer. "Granted that General Dodge will run the line through Tomahawk Pass—but you just heard the Prestons say they wouldn't sell their homesteads at any price. And they'd be doubly hard to deal with if they got an inkling that Gorine was running a survey across their land!" The lawyer smirked. "For once, Delivan, I think you're licked."

The speculator arched his brows and fingered his cravat pin.

"The Prestons refuse to sell," he agreed. "That is where your invaluable talents will come in, DePerren."

Delivan turned to the cinnamon-bearded bartender, who paused in the act of sloshing himself a drink from Bayard's flask. The two men were separated by a gulf as wide as the oceans, so far as culture and education went. Yet Delivan depended on DePerren's lightning-swift guns to back up his own lightning-swift intellect.

"You will start for their ranch tomorrow," said Delivan briskly. "I will accompany you as far as Gorine's survey camp. I'm depending on you to . . . persuade the Prestons to turn Tomahawk Pass over to me."

Linn DePerren unconsciously fingered his gun butt.

"You can count on me, Delivan," assured the gunman.

V

ONE BULLET, ONE VARMINT

QUENT PRESTON, rifle cradled in one buckskin-sleeved elbow and his other hand leading a pack mule, worked his way afoot up through the dwarf aspen and hackberry brush on the north slope of Tomahawk Pass.

Shortly after sunrise that morning, the cowboy had bagged a six-point buck, the carcass of which he had slung under a rock maple near the rim-rock cliffs, and dressed. Venison was scarce at this season, and he was returning with the pack animal to transport the succulent meat down to the Lone Star Ranch cabin.

Reaching the grassy bench where he had stalked the grazing deer, Preston halted to catch his breath after the climb from the valley trail. He expanded his lungs with the winelike mountain air and surveyed the far-flung range with a fierce, possessive pride.

After all, half of those fertile leagues of buffalo grass were his, the rest Panhandle's. It had been hard-won homestead; this had been primitive country when they had trekked out here from Texas three years previously.

Hardship aplenty had dogged them ever since. The years had exacted their toll of sweat and blood and spirit. But now the sloping green trough of Tomahawk Pass had begun to fill with cattle bearing the Lone Star iron. Those steers commanded a price at Laramie and the other army outposts that was double what Texas beef was bringing on the hoof at Abilene or Omaha.

Ideal cow country, this. Beavertail River meandered through the green floor of the pass, fed by the snows which wigged the Sioux Bonnet peaks with silver nine months out of the year, and guaranteed a never-failing source of water for grass and herds.

The pass itself, though rough at its eastern end, provided easy enough exit to outside cattle markets. And by dint of man-breaking labor, the Prestons had reared hay sheds and corrals for the season when ice or snow would make foraging difficult.

Two days had elapsed since he and his father had stumbled accidentally across the U. P. camp at Wagonwheel Springs. It had been good to return to the peace and quiet of the pass. Ellis Bayard's assurance that the railroad would miss their range on its way to Utah had given them a feeling of security and confidence in the freedom of their spread.

Mopping his face with a bandanna, Preston led his flop-eared pack mule across the clearing to where the dressed carcass of the big deer hung from the maple bough. Coyotes had already looted the pile of offal, but the suspended carcass seemed intact.

"In steaks or jerked, this venison will taste plenty *bueno* after all the beef we been eating," Preston commented aloud. "And those antlers won't look bad over the fireplace mant—"

The mule which Preston was in the act of picketing, let out a terrified bray and reared back so violently that it jerked the hackamore out of the Texan's grasp.

The cowboy spun about, knowing well enough that hidden peril lurked near by, to cause the mule to bolt. Even as he lifted his eyes, Preston caught sight of a pair of glittering eyes and slavering rows of fangs up amid the green foliage of the rock maple.

It was the largest panther Quent had ever seen. Spitting a defiant snarl, the beast sprang out into space in a tawny blur of fangs and fur and lashing tail.

With a yell of horror, Preston flung himself to one side. But the screeching varmint's tremendous leap had carried him far over Preston's head and squarely atop the mule, which was in the act of turning tail and bolting for the brush.

The mule went down, even as Preston jumped to pick up his rifle. Great fangs buried deep in the mule's neck, and the beast's hind legs were slashing the mule's white belly to ribbons as a house cat might rip a struggling rat.

Preston swung his .30-.30 to shoulder and pulled the trigger. The roar of the carbine drowned the catamount's humanlike scream of pain, as the steel-jacketed slug bored its way through the panther's flanks, completely piercing its lean body.

But the panther was not mortally hurt. With the uncanny stamina of its breed, the panther wheeled, disregarding the slashed-up mule which lay dying in its own gore, butchered by the panther's terrible claws and fangs.

Preston felt his veins jell with terror as the panther crouched, its eyes blazing green, crimson foam boiling from its fangs as the animal gathered itself to attack a man.

Levering another shell into the breech of the Winchester, Quent Preston backed up as he saw the wounded panther catapult toward him with front paws outstretched, sunlight glinting on distended claws that resembled a bunch of razor blades, any one of which could slash his heart from his body.

Even as the cowboy jerked his rifle up for a pointblank shot at the panther's furry breast, his Mexican spur rowels caught in the buffalo grass and tripped him.

Sprawling on his back, Preston's bullet whined off into the sky. His tumble carried him slightly off the panther's line of flight, but even as his back hit the soft grass Quent Preston felt the animal pounce upon his chap-clad legs.

Claws as sharp as steel hooks ribboned the kangaroo leather boots and thick bullhide chaps as if they were tissue paper. Then the infuriated cat reared on its bloody haunches preparatory to driving its fangs into Quent Preston's throat.

Span! The flat, whiplike crack of a rifle cut through the panther's screech of agony and rage. A heavycalibered bullet drilled the panther's skull, spattering brain matter through the air and extinguishing the green flames in the beast's eyes.

Flopped sideways by the terrific impact of the rifle bullet, the panther's carcass rolled over in the buffalo grass alongside Quent Preston, brown tail whipping the ground, hot blood guttering from its shattered skull.

Wet with sweat, shaken by the nearness of doom but unable to realize what a sheer miracle had saved his life in the last split second before he would have been sliced to hash meat by the berserk animal, Quent Preston climbed groggily to his feet.

He glanced about the scene dazedly, blood dripping from his clothes, his hands palsied. With difficulty he focused his eyes on the threshing hoofs of his pack mule, its belly horribly mutilated by the beast of prey, pitiful brays issuing from a torn throat.

Another rifle shot rang out, and a merciful bullet stilled the pack mule's spasms.

Quent Preston turned his head to where a plume of gun smoke wafted out of the aspen thickets. He was in time to see a lone rider spur into the open, smoke coming from the muzzle of an army carbine.

Leaning shakily on his own rifle, Quent Preston lifted a hand in greeting as the rider dismounted, back turned to the scene.

"Mister, you . . . you sure as hell . . . saved my hide . . . with that expert shootin'!" called out the Texan. "One bullet, one varmint. And thanks for puttin' my poor mule out of its misery. You—"

Quent Preston broke off in amazement, as his rescuer turned from the saddle to face him.

It was no man who had handled that rifle so competently. Chestnut hair flowed from under a Stetson to frame the blue-eyed, smiling face of a girl!

VI

MURDER FROM AMBUSH

SHE was the first woman, aside from Indian squaws, Quent had ever seen in these Sioux Bonnet uplands. This girl was dressed in whipcord riding breeches and mountain boots, and both she and the sorrel she rode struck Preston as familiar.

Then, in a flash of recollection, Quent placed her. This was the girl who had been filling her canteens at Wagonwheel Springs, moments before Cy Trollen's death.

"Why . . . uh—" The Texan started to remove his sombrero, then realized he had lost it when he fell. "How in h—I mean, how come a lone woman would be—"

The girl laughed, and extended a slim, bronzed hand in a grip Preston found as vigorous as a man's.

"I was out for an hour's hunt," she explained. "But this wasn't exactly . . . the sort of hunting I'd planned."

He colored under her merry gaze. "Well, I'm . . . lucky I met up with you when I did," he fumbled. "I'm Quent Preston. You don't live around here, do you?" he added suddenly.

"My name is Helen Gorine," she replied. "My

father has a survey camp over the ridge a mile or so back."

Preston stiffened under the impact of her words.

"A survey camp? Here in Tomahawk Pass?"

She nodded, pointing out over the expanse of country before them, toward the Utah-Wyoming boundary.

"Yes. The Union Pacific will build through this pass to Ogden. Have you ever heard of Major Gorine, the chief surveyor? I'm his daughter. Our camp is just beyond the ridge."

The Union Pacific—building through Tomahawk Pass?

In a voice that was suddenly old, Preston whispered:

"You better ride back to your father's camp, Miss Gorine. Don't think me rude, but . . . but this country ain't safe for a lone girl to be ridin' around in."

"Meaning that I can't take care of myself, Mr. Preston?"

Always reticent in the presence of the other sex, Quent Preston had to grope for words now.

"Of course not. The way you handle a gun— Oh, shucks, Miss Gorine—this country ain't tamed yet. The Sioux are prowlin' these hills, on the prod for scalps because they know this Union Pacific means the end of the buffalo and the Indian."

"I'm not afraid of Indians."

47

"There's rough trappers and prospectors who ain't seen a woman—of your kind—in mebbe years. They'd be worse to meet up with than this varmint you just shot."

Helen Gorine hesitated, then turned and walked back to her horse. When she had mounted and restored her rifle to its saddle scabbard, she said:

"I shan't try to argue the point, Mr. Preston. Do you live in these—dangerous mountains?"

Quent pointed down to where the Lone Star Ranch buildings looked like toys on the bank of Beavertail River, a thousand feet below.

"My father and I own Tomahawk Pass here," he said proudly. "So far, it's wild and lonesome and free out here. We like it that way. Mebbe you could savvy why we aren't hankering for the U. P. to cross through our pass."

Helen Gorine returned his level gaze for several seconds, biting her lip thoughtfully. Then she wheeled her sorrel toward the east.

"Yes. Yes, I believe I do understand," she mused. "But when the railroad does come, you will receive enough right-of-way money to pay you many times over for . . . for what you'll lose."

With a smile of farewell, Helen Gorine spurred off into the scrub maple and conifer growth. The sound of her mount's hoofs died in the distance, and left Quent Preston standing there in the blood-spattered grass, lost in his own thoughts.

He turned away from the scene with a shudder.

He could return later in the day for the deer meat; there was nothing he could do about the matter now, for the buck's carcass was too heavy to tote down the steep mountainside. Timber wolves and buzzards would feast on the panther and the mule, in days to come.

It was an hour before he had regained the valley trail and mounted Alamo, his top pony, a claybank from San Antone. A mile's ride through the trees brought him into the open prairie of Tomahawk Pass, and he spurred into a gallop as he approached the ranch buildings.

A coal-black gelding with a silver-trimmed saddle was tied to the front gate as he arrived. Even as he was tying up Alamo, he heard his father's boots crunching down the gravel path to meet him.

"We got a visitor in there, Quent," announced the whiskery oldster, jerking a thumb to indicate the cabin. "Feller name of DePerren. Come over from Wagonwheel Springs to see if we'd sell out and move."

Quent scowled, adjusting the chin cord of his sombrero.

"You told him neither one of us wanted to sell?"

Panhandle shrugged. "DePerren wouldn't take my no for an answer. Insisted on waitin' till you showed up."

Quent gripped his father's shoulder, his eyes slitting.

"Dad," he said grimly, "this makes two offers we've had to buy this spread. And I've found out why it's so damned popular all of a sudden. The Union Pacific—"

Cr-r-rash! From the half-open doorway of the Lone Star cabin came a spurt of fire and the funneling smoke of a rifle shot.

Panhandle Preston jerked, then tumbled forward into Quent Preston's arms. The rear of his skull was torn away by ambush lead.

VII

TRAIL OF A KILLER

TOO horrified to move a muscle, Quent Preston clung to his father's dead body long enough to see a red-whiskered figure emerge from the doorway, squinting down the barrel of a Winchester.

Again the rifle thundered, and Quent's hat jerked as a slug tunneled his hair and whined off into space.

Caught in the open, the cowboy was at the mercy of DePerren's marksmanship.

Twenty yards away was a small log shack which served as a storage place for tools, a blacksmith's forge, and miscellaneous ranch equipment. A double-barreled shotgun would be in there, for Quent had been carving a new stock for it only yesterday. If he could reach that shack—

Crouching low, Preston sprinted for the shelter of the log wall. A swift spatter of shots came from the cabin, as DePerren dropped to one knee and pumped his rifle lever savagely.

Slugs kicked up geysers of dust under Quent's slogging feet, wailed like banshees past his ears, thudded into the shack's door jamb as the cowboy dived headlong to shelter.

51

He leaped to a workbench, where the shotgun with its unfinished stock was mounted in a vise. With desperate haste the cowboy opened the breech, snatched cartridges from a shelf above the bench and loaded the weapon, then released the buckshot gun from the vise.

Through the open doorway he caught sight of the red-whiskered DePerren advancing cautiously down the path. The outlaw believed he had his victim trapped, for he had seen that Quent wore no belt guns, and his rifle was in his saddle boot.

"Stop where you are, DePerren!"

Preston snarled the order, at the same time thrusting the double-barreled scattergun out the doorway, its twin muzzles covering DePerren.

The outlaw's contorted face went ashen. Then, with a hoarse yell of fear, DePerren headed for his horse. Preston's discharging shotgun sent a blast of shot peppering the gravel pathway where the cinnamon-bearded ambusher had stood, but DePerren had reached his black gelding and was swinging into the saddle before Preston emerged from the workshed.

The shotgun was useless except at short range. Even as DePerren spun his horse about and spurred for the outbound trail, Quent Preston raced into the cabin, flinging the shotgun aside.

Grief and rage were beginning to react. Jerkily, like a sleeper in the meshes of a nightmare, the Texan took a pair of cartridge belts off a wall peg and buckled the gun harness about his lean flanks, adjusting the weight of twin Colts on his thighs.

DePerren had reached the river ford and was splashing across the shallows as Quent Preston emerged from the cabin.

Preston vaulted into saddle, goading his claybank pony with unaccustomed ferocity of spur. Sheets of water erupted from the claybank's flying hoofs as the cowboy sent him across Beavertail River at top gait, and on out over the trail down which DePerren was galloping, half a mile in the distance.

Under Preston's savage lashing, the fast pony had cut down DePerren's lead by a third by the time the outlaw, bending low over the saddle and flinging frequent glances behind him, vanished into the rimming forest.

Alamo galloped with undiminished speed into the lodgepole pines, Quent riding with cold wariness for an ambush, six-gun in hand. This trail was familiar to him; he knew its every twist and turn, whereas DePerren would have to proceed with greater care.

A mile beyond, the trail followed a ledge flanked by precipitous cliffs overlooking the turbulent rapids of Beavertail River. Preston got occasional glimpses of DePerren spurring desperately around bends ahead of him.

Preston's leggy mount was fast overhauling the

outlaw. But each twist of the ledge trail meant the risk of running headlong into DePerren, should the killer choose to shoot it out with his relentless pursuer.

The abyss on the right would shield no one; Quent had only to concentrate on the trail ahead and the dense undergrowth on the left.

Rounding a bend of the ledge, Preston's nostrils suddenly caught the resinous tang of wood smoke. At the same instant he came in view of several canvas tents, pitched in a small clearing a hundred yards ahead.

Because he was concentrating his glance on the unfamiliar encampment ahead, Preston was pitched violently forward when his claybank pony skidded to a halt to keep from colliding with DePerren's horse which blocked the ledge.

DePerren had been forced to dismount to tighten his saddle girth. Now, as Preston thundered around the curving trail, the fleeing outlaw was cornered.

Preston's heart gave a vengeful bound as he swung to the ground, his six-gun covering the red-whiskered rider even as the latter went into a crouch and stabbed spreadout hands toward the swinging stocks of his Colts.

VIII

A DERRINGER DISAPPEARS

GET your arms up, DePerren!"
Preston's cold order drained the color from the killer's face. Staring into the black bore of the Texan's gun, DePerren slowly raised his hands to the level of his flat-crowned Stetson.

"I ought to kill you where you stand," panted the cowboy, as he unbuckled DePerren's gun belts and flung them behind him. "But I ain't that stripe. I'll see you hang—legal—for murdering my father in cold blood."

DePerren seemed to wilt.

"I . . . I . . . was hired to shoot the . . . two of you—" gasped DePerren. "If I stretch rope . . . then—"

A loud drumming of many hoof-beats interrupted DePerren, coming from the direction of the nearby tents. Quent Preston stiffened warily, his eyes lifting to peer at a group of oncoming horsemen beyond the red-whiskered killer.

For an instant Preston wondered if these were friends of the red-whiskered gunman, and then he recognized Boone Delivan and Helen Gorine among the approaching riders, and knew intuitively that the tents belonged to Major Gorine's survey camp.

In the brief heartbeat of time that Preston's attention was diverted from DePerren, the outlaw lowered his right arm to level. With a motion too quick for eye to follow, the red-bearded saloon keeper flicked his wrist.

Magically, the blunt snout of a single-shot .44 derringer slid from its sleeve hide-out, leveled at Quent's head.

Flame spat from the cowboy's heavy revolver. Through pluming gun smoke Preston saw DePerren stagger backward under the churning impact of the bullet which smashed his heart at point-blank range.

The dead outlaw collapsed, the arm holding the unfired sleeve gun extending over the brink of the ledge. As DePerren's fingers flexed spasmodically, the tiny derringer dropped from his grasp and plummeted into the rocks and brush far below.

Preston forgot the oncoming riders, almost upon him now.

With the concussion of his own shot resounding in his eardrums, Quent Preston leaned forward slightly, staring at DePerren's twitching face. The fierce exultation of fulfilled revenge leaped into Preston's blood and intoxicated him with its wild passion.

Then a stern voice cut through his concentration, brought him back to his senses:

"Drop than gun, Preston! You're under military

arrest for the cold-blooded murder of an unarmed man!"

Dazed, Quint Preston looked up to see the trail blocked by riders—seven of them. He recognized the foremost horseman, who held an army rifle trained at his midriff, as Major John Gorine, from his facial resemblance to Helen.

In the rear of Boone Delivan and Helen were cold-eyed surveyors from the U. P. crew, all with drawn six-guns.

Stunned by the turn of events, Quent Preston dropped his smoking .45 and raised his arms. Major Gorine dismounted, handed his reins to Helen. He kept the rifle trained on Preston's chest.

"We witnessed this murder, Preston!" snarled the survey chief. "You killed a defenseless man. And I will see to it that you receive military punishment—death before a firing squad—as quickly as I can get you back to the army post at Wagonwheel Springs!"

It was useless to argue that DePerren's hand had clutched a derringer at the moment of his death. None would believe that Preston had cheated death himself by a shaved instant.

Already, Major Gorine was reaching out with his rifle barrel to unhook the Colt six-gun from Preston's other holster.

And then Quent Preston moved with a speed that was incredible for one of his loose build and careless manner.

Quent's left arm seized the barrel of the surveyor's rifle while his right fist crashed up into Gorine's face.

Yanking the carbine from Gorine's hands as the survey chief reeled back against his horse, Quent Preston flung aside the bulky rifle and got his left-hand Colt from its holster.

Backing grimly toward his own pony, the Texan cocked the .45 to cover the paralyzed figures of the other riders, Helen Gorine among them.

"If any of you move a muscle," snarled Quent Preston as he put boot-toe into stirrup, "I'll shoot to kill!"

IX

DEATH RIDES THE RANGE

THE menace of the six-gun in Quent Preston's hand petrified the seven riders bunched on the ledge trail.

Two of the young surveyors in the rear dropped their weapons with intentionally loud clatters and elevated their hands.

Boone Delivan, his slitted eyes fascinated by the unwavering bore of Preston's weapon, raised his arms as the Texan swung into saddle and picked up his reins with his free hand.

"This may have looked like wanton murder to you-all," drawled Preston, holding a close rein on his restless mount. "But it wasn't. DePerren murdered my father. I chased him three miles—but when I shot him, it was in self-defense."

There was a moment's chilly silence, as Preston curvetted his clay-bank pony broadside to them.

Major Gorine fumbled a trembling hand to his nose, brought it away dyed crimson.

Alone of the tense group, Helen seemed to be in control of her emotions. Her gaze was fixed on DePerren's sprawled corpse.

Major Gorine, recovering his composure long enough to point at the dead man, sneered back:

"This man was unarmed when we saw you kill him. You call that self-defense?"

Preston's ice-blue gaze settled on Helen Gorine, as he answered the unvoiced query in the girl's eyes:

"DePerren pulled a derringer on me—I was lucky to shoot first. You'll find a sleeve holster on DePerren's wrist—it'll be empty. The gun dropped over the cliff edge here."

Major Gorine's goatee trembled with impotent rage.

"You lie, Preston. You disarmed him, then shot him."

Quent Preston started backing his pony toward the bend of the trail leading back to Tomahawk Pass.

"DePerren murdered my father," choked the cowboy. "He died in my arms. I'm going back now—to bury him. I wouldn't advise any of you to follow me."

Rearing his horse as he backed out of sight around the brushy hairpin turn of the ledge trail, Preston vanished from sight. The thud of his horse's galloping hoofs on the pine-needled trail was soon lost in the soft murmur of Beavertail River, plunging down its rocky gorge below.

Major Gorine snatched up his fallen rifle and started down the trail in pursuit, but a sharp cry from Helen made the survey chief check his impulsive chase.

"Don't prod the cowboy, major!" warned Delivan. "He's desperate, now that he realizes his murder was witnessed. We're fortunate he didn't slaughter the bunch of us."

Delivan swung out of stirrups and walked forward, stooping to examine the bullet hole over DePerren's heart. He looked up to see Major Gorine eying him quizzically.

"Who is this DePerren, Boone?" demanded the survey chief. "You and he came to camp last night together."

Delivan stood up, shrugging. Panic was coursing through the speculator's veins, for he had counted on DePerren accomplishing his mission. Quent Preston was alive and free, and with a heart filled with hate and revenge. Such a man would be a dangerous adversary in a game as desperate as the one Delivan was playing.

"You know him as well as I do," lied the speculator gravely. "I met him for the first time on the trail, coming to your camp. He said he was riding out to Tomahawk Pass to look at a cattle ranch he planned to buy. That's all I know about him."

The four surveyors and Helen Gorine had dismounted and were now grouped about the red-bearded corpse. Major Gorine stooped, feeling under DePerren's left sleeve. He drew out a loaded .44-caliber derringer with a shiny cedar handle. The dead man's other wrist also bore

61

concealed holster harness—but this, as Quent Preston had told them, was significantly empty.

"This might indicate," mused the major reflectively, "that DePerren *was* resisting when we saw Preston shoot him. Men who are cowardly enough to carry hide-out guns often shoot with amazing dexterity."

Boone Delivan glanced about uneasily.

"I am returning to end of track this afternoon, major," he said. "If you wish, I can take DePerren's personal effects back to Wagonwheel and do what I can to locate any relatives he may have left behind. I presume it would be best to bury him out here, and mark the grave."

Major Gorine fingered his battered nose broodingly.

"The army is the only law and order with jurisdiction here in Wyoming," he muttered. "I will send a letter by you, Boone, to Lieutenant Colonel Sires at Wagonwheel, advising him about this murder. It will be their responsibility to arrest Preston, not mine."

For the first time, Helen Gorine put in a word.

"You'll do no such thing, dad. If DePerren murdered Preston's father, this killing was justifiable. Especially as there seems to be proof that Mr. Preston shot in self-defense."

Boone Delivan's eyes flickered over the girl in surprise.

"Why should you defend this cowboy?" he

62

demanded. "Or do you feel a maternal interest in him, having rescued him today?"

Helen's eyes flashed defiantly at his accusing tone.

"Why should you be so anxious to see him face a firing squad?" she flared. "And another thing, Boone—do you swear you never saw this DePerren before you met him on the trail yesterday coming here?"

The speculator colored, then regained his composure.

"Of course. He was a total stranger to me. Why should you ask me that, dear?"

Major Gorine cut in impatiently:

"Helen, go back to your camp at once. Delivan, you have my permission to assemble the dead man's effects. In the meantime we'll be getting a grave ready."

Helen Gorine, her eyes flooded with sudden tears, fled to the shelter of her private tent and flung herself on an army cot.

Boone Delivan had asked her to marry him when the U. P. was finished. He had repeated his proposal only the night before.

But some instinctive suspicion of the smooth-voiced speculator, some feeling not quite definite, had made her postpone any certain answer to his proposal of marriage.

Now, more strongly than ever, doubt had come to prick her innermost heart. Distrust was

63

emphasized amid a strong sense of disillusionment toward Boone Delivan.

Her memory went back vividly to that eventful morning at the construction camp when Delivan had cowed a lynch mob to rescue the Prestons. As she rode out of town that day she remembered having turned in saddle to wave a last farewell to the man she admired most.

But Delivan hadn't been looking her way. He was walking into Ellis Bayard's office with a red-bearded man. That man had been DePerren, who now lay dead out on the trail, accused of murder by Quent Preston!

"Boone lied—he said he'd never met the man before yesterday—Why? Why?" she asked herself desperately.

Peering out through the flap of the tent, she saw her father handing Delivan an envelope—an official report to the army commander regarding Quent Preston's shooting scrape. She saw Delivan mount his horse and call out to her:

"I'm leaving, Helen. I'll be back next week with your mail. Is there anything I can bring you from town?"

She made no reply, burying her face in her pillow with a sob.

It was dark by the time Boone Delivan had traversed the forty-five miles back to Wagonwheel Springs. The wild night life of the boom town was already starting. An army of Irish railroad workers had returned from the tracks to crowd the saloons and gambling dens.

Raucous music issued from garish dance halls, filling the humid dusk with strident discord.

Delivan turned his winded horse over to a hostler at a canvas-roofed livery barn, and headed off through the alleylike lanes weaving amid the lamp-lighted tents, making his way to the southern edge of the town where the regiment of United States cavalry had its barracks.

Delivan's brain had been busy during the hard afternoon's ride back out of the Sioux Bonnets. DePerren's death had thrown a huge monkey wrench into the well-oiled machinery of the speculator's plans to get title to Tomahawk Pass. But Delivan was used to bucking odds and overcoming them, however great.

The climax of his career lay before him, in the acquisition of the strategically-situated pass. He knew that Quent Preston would be impossible to deal with in a business way, whether the cowboy got an inkling of the new value of his homestead or not.

DePerren had somehow failed to put the Prestons, father and son, out of the picture for all time. What had transpired at the Lone Star Ranch, Delivan could not fathom. But he saw his way clear in the way events were shaping up, anyway.

"A military court will make short work of Quent Preston," muttered Delivan, as he strode off across a drill ground whose sagebrush clumps were already flattened by parading horses. "Ellis Bayard can forge title papers to the Tomahawk Pass right of way easily enough. With Preston out of the way—"

Boone Delivan's work on the Union Pacific project would be done. He would have milked his last penny of profit out of the transcontinental tracks. He welcomed the opportunity to rake in his final pot, toss the cards on the table, and move on to conquer fresh fields.

There would be California—a decade past the heyday of its gold rush, but still teeming with wealth to be plucked from the unwary.

Five minutes later found Boone Delivan delivering Major Gorine's letter to Colonel Sires' staff of army officers in the cavalry headquarters building.

Speaking as a disinterested outsider obeying John Gorine's orders, Delivan recounted his own story of the death of Linn DePerren, also mentioning the fact that Quent Preston had been the slayer of Cyrus Trollen at the waterhole only a few days before.

"Gorine is depending on you to arrest this Preston," wound up the speculator, picking up his hat. "I don't blame him—his surveyors will be working on Preston's ranch in a few days."

The silvery-haired lieutenant colonel scanned Gorine's letter and shook his head gravely.

"In spite of Gorine's belief that Preston is guilty of a foul murder," said the army officer slowly, "it is impossible for me to send a man up there to apprehend him. Doubtless Preston will escape the country, anyway."

"But Gorine is depending—"

"It is impossible, Delivan. I can't spare a single soldier from camp—not with the Indian danger what it is. Only today my scouts told me of a concentration of Sioux warriors not fifty miles away. They may attack the railroad gangs at any moment. Our first duty is to protect the U. P.— not police this wilderness every time there is a shooting."

Delivan's eyes did not mirror the disappointment that surged through his body at Sires' refusal to enter the Preston case.

"I can understand perfectly, sir. And now, if that is all the service I can be, I will bid you good night."

X

THE WORLD ABLAZE

FOR three tense days, Quent Preston went about his duties on the Lone Star Ranch with guns belted on his hips and his pony always within reach.

But thus far, no delegation of men had come to his ranch to arrest him.

He had laid his father to rest down by the river's edge, on a grassy patch where he and Panhandle had pitched their first night's camp in Tomahawk Pass.

He recalled how the old Texan had seated himself on a flat block of gypsum, and had waved a gnarled hand at the beauty of the rimming Sioux Bonnets. His words had anchored them to Wyoming soil from that moment forward:

"This is the spot, Quent. Here's what we been hunting. We'll prove up on this range, starting now. O. K.?"

That blue gypsum boulder was Panhandle's monument now. With a hammer and chisel, Quent cut a tragic legend into the rock by the oblong mound of fresh earth:

QUENTIN PRESTON
MAY HIS SOUL
FIND ELBOW ROOM

As the copper globe of the sun disappeared behind the flat Utah horizon on the third night after Panhandle's murder, Quent Preston made his way to the lonely cabin and cooked supper, trying to forget the haunting presence of the companion who had always taken charge of skillet and coffeepot.

"Gorine hasn't dared come after me yet," muttered Quent, as he shucked his boots that evening and hung his gun belts on a rawhide-bottomed chair near his bunk. "If they were going to push that murder charge against me, they'd have been here by now."

Quent had driven himself to the limit of his endurance that day with work around the ranch. Only by severe manual labor could he stamp from his mind the ghastly memory of Panhandle's collapse in his arms, a bullet in his head.

Pulling a buffalo robe over himself to keep out the night chill, Preston slept. So sound was his slumber that no nightmares came to torture his dreams as on previous nights.

Thus he did not hear the uneasy trumpeting of his cavvy of saddle horses out in the corral, shortly after midnight.

Phantom moonlight disclosed a scene that would have spelled "Indian attack!" to Preston, had he been wakened by the horses.

For over on the north bank of Beavertail River, the ghostly shapes of eight horsemen moved slowly in Indian file along the rim of the prairie.

There they divided, four heading off toward the open range where the Lone Star beef herd were bedded for the night.

The remaining four spurred their fleet ponies down into the river where it sluiced over a gravel bar, and slowly forded the stream, so as not to make noise.

Reaching the south bank, the quartet melted into a bosque of willow and salt cedar, where they tied their mounts.

Minutes later they slunk stealthily up the cut bank to vanish behind a low haystack near the Preston barn.

Half an hour later, Quent Preston sat bolt upright in his bunk, the acrid tang of fresh smoke biting his nostrils.

It was one A.M. by the battered alarm clock on the table.

A sinister pink glow outlined the rectangle of his windows.

"Hey, dad—wake up! Our range must be afire—"

Quent broke off, as memory returned to tell him that his father's bunk was forever empty. The awful emptiness of the cabin closed about him as he groped in the darkness for his spurred cow-boots.

Not pausing to strap on his cartridge belts, Preston raced across the floor and flung open the door. Then he sagged back against the door jamb, as his eyes beheld a fantastic and awful spectacle. It seemed as if the entire world were a blazing inferno.

Across the river, lurid flames were leaping skyward along a three-mile front—flames that filled the night with a crackling roar that drowned the familiar song of the Beavertail sluicing over its rapids.

Billowing mountains of pink and white smoke blotted out the moon and stars. A stiff night wind, whipping off the Sioux Bonnet peaks, was pushing the grass fire across thousands of acres of unfenced range faster than a man could run.

Faintly to Quent's dazed eardrums came the far-off bellow of frantic cattle, the rumble of cloven hoofs—sounds of stampede that faded and were soon lost behind the ominous thunder of the prairie fire.

Sparks hurtled across the river in a crimson barrage. Already, dry grass was igniting on the ranch side of the Beavertail, small fires which the wind would quickly spread into an uncontrollable conflagration.

Despair paralyzed the cowboy as his ears caught the panicked whiskers of his ten saddle horses, crazed by the sullen roar of the prairie fire and the blast of superheated air which was rapidly making life unendurable even at this distance from the fire.

"I got to save my broncs—if the wind changes these barns will go—everything will go—"

Preston headed down the front yard path toward the corral gates, to free the milling horses. They could gain the shelter of upper slopes if left to themselves, and could be rounded up if—

A bullet kicked gravel on Preston's boots. Two more slammed into the door behind him before he had taken two forward strides.

"Shots! What in hell—"

The cowboy slid to a halt, his brain for the moment unable to comprehend the dull, whipcrack reports of fast-triggered rifles.

Then the hornetlike whine of a bullet bare inches from his head drove comprehension into Preston's mind.

"It's an Injun raid! The Sioux are burning me out!"

Preston dropped to his belly and scuttled for the refuge of the cabin door. It took an eternity to traverse the few feet he had covered, and bullets peppered the ground and steps about him before he was over the threshold.

Gasping like a landed fish, Quent Preston leaped up and slammed shut the heavy slab door. Then he ran for his guns.

The inside of the cabin, hazy now with drifting smoke, was illuminated as bright as day by the hellish wall of fire that was devastating his range grass. He caught a glimpse of his reflected image in the window glass, and saw the face drawn tight, eyes wide with horror.

Even as he looked, the windowpane was obliterated by the crash of bullets that punctured a hanging skillet over the range and slammed off the iron stove with clangs like a fire bell.

"Thank God—dad never lived to see the Sioux attack the ranch. Dad always believed the Injuns were our friends."

XI

SILENT SANCTUARY

WITH hands that were once more steady, Quent Preston groped over the door for his Winchester, racked on two sets of antlers.

He took it down, levered a cartridge into the barrel, then dropped to one knee and poked sphagnum-moss chinking out from between two logs.

A hot blast of air whistled through the crack. Squinting against the smoke, Quent peered outside, his eyes sweeping the entire front of the river bank.

No trace of skulking, feather-bonneted Sioux did the cowboy see. But that was natural. Indians could hide themselves with the uncanny skill of quail. They had fired his range, knowing that would bring him out into the open.

Always the most friendly relations had existed between the Prestons and the Sioux who roamed the Wyoming badlands. They had traded goods, horses, even shared food with tribal chieftains inside this very cabin. The Sioux had smoked the pipe of peace with Panhandle Preston and Quent, more than once. Yet tonight—

It struck Quent as odd that he heard no Indian war whoops. It was also queer that no flaming arrows had come out of the night to set fire to the sod roof of his cabin. Then Quent Preston caught sight of a darting figure emerging from behind a strawstack that had suddenly burst into flames. Through the twisting coils of smoke Preston could make out no details. But his imagination pictured a naked savage, sprinting on moccasined feet toward the river.

Drawing a quick bead, Quent pulled trigger, saw the fleeing enemy throw up his hands and pitch face foremost into the dirt.

Preston swore through clenched teeth. He had drawn first blood in a fray that he knew must end with death for himself. It was a question of minutes before the sod roof of his cabin would catch fire from blowing sparks. That would convert the cabin into a bake oven, force him into the open to be cut down by Sioux marksmen.

Glass showered in a musical crash over the kneeling cowboy as a rain of bullets demolished the window overhead. Logs thudded under the impact of leaden missiles, and in the sake of prudence Quent deserted his position and scuttled to the back wall.

Again knocking out chinking moss, Preston studied the flame-lighted back yard of his ranchhouse. A crash of splintering wood told him that his horses were leaping over the cavvy corral pen.

A moment later he saw two of his own string

and one of Panhandle's mustangs galloping off to vanish in the smoke. He recognized Alamo, his prize claybank.

It was strange that the Indians had not raided his horse corral before firing the range. Horses and guns were the booty of raiding Sioux, especially since they needed all the resources possible in their warfare against the Union Pacific builders.

"The railroad! The damned railroad—it's responsible for the Injuns burning me out tonight!"

Quent screamed the words out of a throat that was getting dry and parched.

"The Sioux have declared war on all whites—they haven't anything against me—that damned U. P. goaded them into it!"

It was unbearable, crouching here in a doomed cabin with no target to vent his wrath upon. And then, above the deep roar of the prairie fire, came a sharp crackle of flames near at hand.

Preston hauled his rifle barrel out from between the logs and looked overhead. A thousand lurid tongues of flames were fast consuming the sod which shingled his pole-raftered roof.

Torturing waves of heated air smote the cowboy, drying the sweat which leaked from his pores. For ten minutes he endured the stinging smoke that was clogging his lungs, making it impossible to see across the cabin.

"I got . . . to get outdoors . . . or be roasted alive—"

Crawling on his belly across the floor, Preston paused by the table in midroom long enough to fill his pockets with .30-.30 ammunition from a box on the table.

Then he got to his feet and fought his way through falling cinders and unbreathable smudge until his hand encountered the rawhide latchstring of the door.

It was suicide to go out, but a worse death to remain until the roof caved in over him. Bracing his body against an expected deluge of bullets or feather-tipped arrows, Preston flung open the door and headed into the open.

An outward-gushing wave of white smoke from the cabin shielded him as he headed for the river, head down, legs slogging. Now he could breathe. If he could reach the river there was a faint chance of escaping Indian attackers by floating downstream, hiding in the willows.

Then, dim and ghostly through the flame-tinged smoke, Quent Preston saw his trail blocked by a looming figure.

Even as he whipped up his rifle and fired at the oncoming foe, the cowboy saw that the man wore a cone-peaked Stetson instead of a top-knot feather or a bannering Sioux war bonnet.

The two fired together, at point-blank range. But the raider's shot went wild, even as Preston's slug drilled his neck and dropped him, dead before he hit the ground.

As Preston vaulted over the dead man, he confirmed what he had seen. His foe was no striped, copper-skinned Indian warrior. He was a bearded white man!

"Then—this ain't an Indian attack—"

Gagging for breath, Quent vaulted a blue gypsum boulder and crouched down on a mound of fresh-spaded earth where the air was fresher.

He had sought refuge on his father's grave.

XII

OUT OF HELL, A CONFESSION

HOARSE yells came out of the tortured night, yells which put to rest any lingering doubt which Preston might have had regarding the fact that Sioux warriors were playing no part in tonight's holocaust.

"I tell yuh, Preston left the cabin!"

"Then he's headed for the river—we got to separate."

Preston scuttled forward over his father's grave mound and rested his hot-barreled rifle on the smooth surface of the gypsum tombstone.

Gone was the blank feeling of despair that had killed his fighting spirit inside the cabin. Possibly his nearness to Panhandle's resting place inspired him; his blood ran hot with a compelling desire to kill, a ruthless determination to destroy the renegades who had made a shambles of his homestead and were even now questing for his life.

He saw no trace of the men who had exchanged yells.

His cabin was ablaze from roof-tree to foundation blocks. With it was being consumed the fruits and hopes of three years of toil. All

79

that he and Panhandle had accomplished was represented in that sturdy log cabin that had been their home here in the wilderness.

Then, silhouetted against the ruby glare of the flame, near the shrouded house, Quent Preston caught sight of two burly figures heading at top speed down the sloping yard toward the river.

The two spotted Preston at the same instant. One of the raiders ducked at right angles for the shelter of a stone well coaming. The other knelt to aim his rifle at the cowboy behind the tombstone.

Preston shot the latter without aiming, saw the man sprawl kicking. Then he swung his rifle, lining the sights to cover the sprinting raider who was triggering a Colt in his direction.

Even as the killer dived for the stone well housing, Quent fired. The man staggered, bullet-hit, then vanished behind the well. Whether he was mortally wounded, the cowboy could not tell.

Smoke beat down in billowing waves, forcing Preston to seek the refuge of the nearby river. As he slid down the short pitch of shale to the water's edge he saw a heavy-set rider fording the shallow stream, swerving in his direction.

"That you, Averill?" called the raider, as his horse splashed up the shelving bank. "I move we head for Wagonwheel. Preston's beef herd is scattered from hell to breakfast, and—"

In the act of dismounting alongside Preston, the horseman caught the full brunt of the cowboy's rifle barrel across the temple. He tumbled backward, falling against Preston and landing on his back in the shallow water.

Preston unbuckled a lariat coil from the pommel of the raider's saddle and quickly lashed the unconscious man's wrists behind his back, then trussed his legs securely at knee and ankle.

That done, the cowboy refreshed himself with the cool water, then scrambled back up the cut bank to resume his vigil behind Panhandle's gravestone.

An eternity of waiting followed. He saw no more skulking raiders, heard no yells or gunshots. The volcano-like noise of the night began to diminish as the prairie fire hurried westward like a tidal wave of red destruction.

One by one the screams of smothering horses sounded in the corral, as the animals perished. Then the main barn collapsed with a roar of fire-eaten studding and rafters!

Dawn found Quent Preston, gaunt and spent, atop his father's grave mound. A providential shift of the wind had halted the prairie fire shortly before sunrise, miles west of the ranch.

As day stole over Tomahawk Pass, a high breeze from the snow-blanketed crags dissolved the smoke which clogged the valley from rimrock to rimrock.

Sore in every muscle, Preston walked out over

grass that was burned to the very roots, to survey the carnage about him.

The lifting sun looked down on a scene that was indescribable in its utter devastation.

Heaps of blazing embers marked the Lone Star buildings. The blackened fireplace chimney of the cabin seemed like a tomb over Quent's dead hopes.

He turned to survey the opposite side of the river. His prime longhorn steers had grazed there the day before. Not one was in sight now; they would be hopelessly scattered out onto the western desert, fleeing before the greedy advance of the fire.

The beautiful prairie of yesterday was now blackened ruin. Skeletons of once-magnificent live oaks dotted the plain. The pine forest to the north bristled with smoking snags, the timber having been gutted clean to the very foot of the cliffs which had kept the conflagration confined to the pass itself.

Preston walked on, drawn irresistibly toward the corpse of the first raider he had encountered on his dash from the blazing cabin. Flames had singed off the dead man's beard, revealing an evil, contorted face beneath. Fire still smoldered on the bloodstained fabric of his shirt. The odor of fried flesh was revolting in the cowboy's nostrils.

Yet no sense of pity or regret stirred him. The

four men who had felt the vengeance of his rifle were no doubt but a part of the gang of raiders who had engineered the night's havoc.

"Dad didn't live to see this," he choked out despondently. "That's the only good thing—that I can see in this hell."

The fire which had annihilated the Lone Star seemed also to have burned out the core of Preston's heart. He moved like a puppet, staring emptily out over the desolation about him with only a numb despair in his being.

A groan roused him out of his torpor. He looked around, then saw the raider who had gained the shelter of the well housing. The man still lived; he had crawled to the well and was trying to reach a water bucket that rested on the stone casing.

Striding swiftly forward, Quent stared down at the dying outlaw as the latter panted hoarsely:

"Water, pard. I'm playin' out my string . . . give me drink."

Quent laughed, in the berserk fashion of an insane person.

"Suffer, damn your black soul! Lie there and suffer with a bullet in your belly! No water do you get from me—"

The dying man slumped back, pressing a bullet-drilled side with a gore-plastered hand. His gaze crossed Preston's again, but the pleading had gone out of them.

"I don't blame . . . you a damn bit . . . Preston."

The cowboy swore under his breath and looked down into the well, its sparkling surface littered with fine-sifted ashes. Then, lowering the bucket with a fire-scorched rope, Quent brought it up, dripping and icy cool.

Kneeling beside the wounded killer, Preston held the rim of the water bucket to the man's lips, watched him gulp avidly.

"Drink, damn you. I won't lower myself to your stripe by refusing water to a man headed for hell."

Spent by the effort of propping himself up, the crook sagged back, his eyes clinging to Preston's bitter countenance.

"I ain't . . . the man you're after . . . Preston," he whispered. "I'm just . . . a flunky who rents . . . his guns. But I'm glad . . . we didn't tally you."

Preston's bleak eyes did not change expression.

"I'm Bob . . . Averill," choked the raider. "I was boss . . . of this bonfire party. But my boss . . . who paid us . . . he's the hombre you want."

Preston's eyelids widened, as if his brain was thinking clearly again.

"Your boss?—Is the Union Pacific behind this, Averill? Did they send you here to wipe me out so they could build their damned railroad across my range?"

Averill's voice came in a gusty croak. Life was already ebbing rapidly from his pain-bright eyes:

"Not . . . Union Pacific . . . directly. My gun boss . . . Boone Delivan—"

Every nerve and fiber in Quent Preston's body came tingling to life as Averill finished speaking to go into a paroxysm of coughing. His blood raced, fueled by the fires of hate that seethed through his heart.

"You say Boone Delivan was behind last night's raid, Averill?"

Drawn and white and spent, Averill nodded. "Delivan . . . yes. Hard man . . . out to break you—"

Once more Bob Averill lifted a feeble hand toward the water bucket. But he was dead before Quent Preston could lift it to his crimson-flecked mouth again.

XIII

IN QUEST OF VENGEANCE

A CLATTER of hoofbeats on black-baked soil
made Quent Preston leap violently to his
feet, guns in hand. But it was not the other
members of Boone Delivan's raiding party who
were approaching.

Instead, Quent's favorite pony, Alamo, was
cantering down the slope, heading for the river.
Behind the claybank came the other two
mustangs who had escaped the fire-girdled corral
the night before.

With a glad cry of welcome, Preston strode
out after the three horses. Then he returned to
untie the well's bucket rope, and fashioned a
hackamore loop out of the wet hemp as he
strode down to the river bank. There he had no
difficulty in dropping the noose over Alamo's
nose.

The pony shied in sudden alarm, and for the
first time since sunrise Preston remembered the
outlaw he had trussed up by the river bank.

The hombre was sitting up now, his boot-clad
legs still submerged in the rippling stream. A pair
of spark-bright eyes narrowed as Preston walked
up, leading his horse.

"What's your name?"

86

The whiskery-faced crook licked his lips nervously.

"Weldon—But you ain't got anything on me, Preston. I didn't have a hand in guttin' your spread last night."

Preston unholstered a six-gun and hefted its weight ominously. The action made Weldon's countenance go chalky-white.

"I got a mind to kill you where you're sittin', Weldon. But I got a hunch you're goin' to come in handy when I haul Boone Delivan before a military court in Wagonwheel."

At mention of Delivan's name, Weldon stiffened perceptibly in his bonds. Then he relaxed with a leer.

"I never heard o' Boone Delivan."

Preston's thumb idly cocked the knurled hammer of his .45.

"Bob Averill talked—before he died," said the Texan coldly. "But since you won't co-operate and try to save your own hide—I guess I'll have to—"

Weldon recoiled frantically as Preston drew deliberate aim at his forehead.

"No—don't shoot, Preston. I'll talk—plenty. I'll talk Boone Delivan onto the gallows. But me—I never killed a man in my life. I never set fire to your range."

Preston shrugged, and holstered his gun. Removing a cattle knife from his chaps pocket, he bent down and cut the bonds which pinioned Weldon's legs.

"Start walking, Weldon. We're heading for Wagonwheel pronto. I ain't giving Boone Delivan a chance to skip."

A vigorous whickering from the vicinity of a bosque of salt cedars a few yards away directed Preston's attention to the four saddled-and-bridled horses of the dead outlaws. Sight of them brought a grin of triumph to the Texan's lips.

"There's saddles for my pony and the one you'll ride, Weldon," grunted Preston with satisfaction. "I'll help you mount."

Five minutes later they were riding up the cut bank, Weldon in front on a horse whose brand showed him to have been the property of Bob Averill. Preston's claybank was rigged with a swellfork Brazos saddle to replace his own battered hull that had been lost in the fire.

Wheeling Alamo to the eastward, Quent Preston set off toward the cool green timber that encroached upon the now-barren prairie. Weldon, his arms still bound behind his back, rode at Preston's stirrup, a hackamore leading to the cowboy's saddlehorn to make sure the raider would make no attempt at escape.

When they had reached the last place along the river where they could make a crossing, Preston reined up.

"We dassn't keep on this trail or we'd pass

Gorine's survey camp," he told Weldon. "That'd be beggin' trouble. We'll take the old deer trail across the river."

The horses plunged into the Beavertail's icy flood until the stirrups were submerged. Then the ford shallowed off and the cowboy and his prisoner were heading up the steep bank.

A weed-grown but clearly defined game trail opened up through the towering pines about them, wide enough for the two to ride abreast.

The weight of heavy Frontier Colts on his chap-clad thighs slopped slowly against the jolting of his horse. Back in Texas he had never worn those matched .45s in his daily work. But now they seemed an integral part of him.

"Boone Delivan's probably a wizard with guns. Or maybe he's a derringer expert like DePerren. Leastwise I'll be plenty cagey when we cross trails tonight."

Thought of the burned-over desolation behind him forced hot blood to the cowboy's face. He pressed Weldon for details, but the prisoner lapsed into sullen silence which no amount of threatening could break.

But recent happenings were beginning to stand out in their true perspective, now that Boone Delivan's name was linked to his misfortune. Preston had no doubt but that the ruffian DePerren had been sent out to Tomahawk Pass with orders to murder both his father and himself.

DePerren's failure had resulted in last night's raid.

Suddenly both horses reared back violently, so that Preston had to grab the saddle horn to keep his seat. Getting the pony under control and leaning from saddle to check the bucking of Weldon's mount, Preston caught sight of the object that had startled the horses.

It was a glittering instrument of brass, mounted on a hardwood tripod and standing amid the low fernbrake by the trailside not a dozen feet away.

"A surveyor's transit."

Even as Quent identified the instrument, a harsh command rang like a thunderclap through the silence of the vast forest:

"Hands up, Preston! You're under a triple drop!"

Preston raised his arms tentatively and peered about. His glance surprised a triumphant grin on Weldon's face, and for an instant his heart sank before the possibility of having run into the other raiders who had fired his grassland.

Then, from out of a pile of broken talus rocks bordering the uphill side of the trail, stepped Major John Gorine, once more holding the cowboy in the threat of his rifle sights.

Out of the ferns on the opposite side of the trail stepped two men whom Preston recognized as the young surveyors who had witnessed his shooting of DePerren.

Flight or resistance would be suicidal. In a dead voice, Preston said:

"I won't get spooky, Gorine. Take it easy with those guns."

One of the engineers hurried up to seize the bridles of the two horses. All three of the U. P. crew were staring at Weldon curiously, noting the fact that his arms were bound.

"Dismount, Preston. We caught sight of the two of you a mile away, through our transit telescope. I didn't think you'd have the nerve to stick around this country."

Preston slid from stirrups and felt the third surveyor remove his .45s from their holsters.

"What can you tell us about the Indian situation, Preston?" asked Gorine anxiously. "With Helen in camp, I—That is, we saw the sky reddened by that fire last night and we knew the Sioux must have attacked your range."

Preston's lips curved in a brittle smile.

"You railroaders blamed the Sioux for that fire, eh? To put you at ease regarding your daughter's safety, I'll say that there hasn't been a redskin in the Sioux Bonnets for weeks. They're all out on the plains, battling your Iron Horse."

"Then who set fire—"

Preston jerked a thumb toward Weldon.

"Ask Weldon, my prisoner. He's one of a gang of raiders who wiped my homestead clean and spread my beef herd from hell to breakfast—all

91

so that his boss could grab my range and sell it to your damned U. P.!"

Major Gorine's jaw sagged on an oath of astonishment. He glanced up at the whiskery-jowled outlaw and demanded harshly:

"What's Preston talking about? Who hired you to burn up Preston's range? What's the U. P. got to do with it?"

Weldon stirred uneasily in his saddle.

"Boone Delivan hired Bob Averill's saloon gang to break Preston. But I didn't have any part—*aaargh!*"

As Quent Preston stared aghast, he saw Weldon's body jerk under the terrific impact of a bullet in the back. Death glazed the raider's eyes as he bent forward over the pommel, blood coursing out over his trussed-together arms.

From high on the mountainside came the thin, jarring report of a high-calibered rifle.

Staring off beyond Weldon's tottering corpse, Preston saw three horsemen outlined sharply against the sky on the craggy rimrock hundreds of feet above.

And in that moment, Quent Preston knew why they had shot Weldon. They were the remaining members of last night's raiding party—and their bullet had killed Preston's only witness to prove the guilt of Boone Delivan.

XIV

BUSINESS IN WAGONWHEEL

SMOKE puffed from one of the rimrock trio's rifles, and a second bullet screamed down out of space to ricochet off a boulder almost in line with Preston's body.

"Quick—hide in those rocks!" yelled the Texan, lunging forward as if oblivious to the guns trained upon him. "They're gunning for me *now*—you'll all be bushwhacked!"

Yanking Alamo's reins as he dived, Preston gained the shelter of the boulder nest which had concealed Major Gorine. The three engineers scrambled to safety, ducking instinctively as high-calibered slugs whined spitefully all about them.

Weldon's corpse toppled from the saddle before Preston could haul at the hackamore rope to bring the dead man's horse off the trail.

Scuttling on hands and knees to the edge of a gigantic talus boulder, Preston looked up at the rimrock to see the three riders curvette their horses and disappear from view.

From that point on the shoulder of Tomahawk Pass the trio had commanded a view of both trails leading out of the Pass. It was plain that they had posted themselves there to guard against the eventuality of Quent Preston showing up alive.

"Those hombres up there," explained the cowboy as he turned back to Major Gorine, "were in Delivan's raiding party last night, Gorine. And they cooked my chances of proving Delivan is a crook when they shot Weldon—with a bullet intended for me."

Major Gorine gave vent to a low groan of disillusionment as he lowered his rifle.

"I . . . I can't hold you, after what Weldon said," whispered the survey chief in a shaky tone. "Henderson, give Preston back his guns. I . . . I guess I was mistaken in you, Preston."

Preston took his Frontier .45s from the young engineer and replaced them in his holsters with a taut smile.

"I'm beginning to see—the reason for Boone's visits to my survey camps," husked the engineer. "I thought he came out to pay court to Helen. Now I can see it was a ruse to gain information about my survey through Tomahawk Pass. He tried to get you out of the way so he could get title to your homestead and sell right of way to the Union Pacific."

Preston bit his lip thoughtfully. A new course of action had been suggested by the old engineer's words, a plan to beat Delivan at his own game.

"Gorine," said the Texan, "Delivan had me licked last night. I'm broke. It'll take money to

94

rebuild my place and stock my range with cattle again. Tell me—is the U. P. really going to run through Tomahawk Pass?"

Gorine straightened, pride making his eyes flash.

"Absolutely. I stake my reputation as an engineer on the certainty that General Dodge will order the U. P. R. through this route."

Preston stared off through the trees, lost in thought.

"What would happen," the cowboy wanted to know, "if I refused to sell right of way through my homestead?"

Gorine put a big hand on Preston's shoulder.

"Preston, you'd be bucking something bigger than you are. The Union Pacific is big—stupendous. The government is behind it. The destiny of America is wrapped up in it. Your land would be condemned by the courts and the U. P. would go on, regardless of your attitude."

"How much would the U. P. pay me for right of way?"

Gorine paused to consider.

"A legitimate price would be at least twenty thousand dollars. Possibly more, considering the strategic position of your land. The U. P.'s Credit Mobilier has millions in capital behind it."

As if he had reached a momentous decision, Quent Preston squared his shoulders and took a hitch in his belts.

He turned on his heel, swung aboard his

claybank pony and undallied the lead rope connected to Weldon's horse.

"Where are you going?" demanded Gorine anxiously.

The cowboy smiled, but it was not a pleasant smile.

"To Wagonwheel Springs. On business."

"You intend to negotiate with the U. P. R. about right of way?"

Preston was already out in the trail, headed east.

"Yes. I'm going to get that business lined up— and then I'm going to hunt down Boone Delivan!"

Gorine lifted a shaking hand, but Quent Preston had roweled his claybank saddler into a gallop and was already disappearing down the tree-flanked trail.

The chief surveyor turned to his sober-faced assistants.

"Carry on until quitting time, boys," Major Gorine said dully. "Maybe you'd better bury this man. I'm going back to camp. The shape my mind's in, I couldn't read a compass or manage a plumb bob."

Helen Gorine was boiling a kettle of potatoes over the open campfire when her father reached camp an hour later. She glanced up in alarm, surprised both by the major's early return from the field and by the gray look on his face.

"Is anything wrong, dad?" she questioned, running to his side.

Her father took Helen's shoulders in his gnarled hands and drank strength from the love in her gaze.

"My little girl," he whispered, "I don't like to tell you this, but I believe you ought to know. It's about Delivan—"

The girl did not flinch.

"Boone—something has happened to him?"

Taking a deep breath, Major Gorine recounted swiftly his arrest of Quent Preston on the trail, and the startling revelation which the outlaw, Weldon, had given just before an ambush bullet had plunged him into eternity.

A sigh that was almost one of relief came from the girl, as he pressed her cheek against his shoulder.

"Dad," she said, "I already knew—about Boone."

And she told him of Delivan's lie regarding DePerren, a lie which had taken on sinister implications as a result of subsequent happenings.

"Where . . . where is Quent Preston now!" she asked, moving back from her father's arms. "You . . . you let him go free, didn't you?"

Major Gorine nodded heavily.

"Of course. The last I saw of him, he was riding to Wagonwheel Springs, to start negotiations with

97

the Union Pacific for the sale of right of way. And then he said he was going to look up Boone Delivan. I . . . I didn't like the way he said that."

Stark fear sprang into Helen Gorine's eyes.

"Dad!" she cried, clutching his arms. "Preston intends to kill Delivan! It's the way men do things out here. Dad, we've got to ride to Wagonwheel today—now! We've got to stop Preston!"

Major Gorine grunted half-heartedly as Helen started dragging him toward the horse corral.

"The way I feel now," confessed her father, "I wouldn't care much—if Preston did kill Delivan. It would be justice."

"No . . . no!" she cried back through the dust. "They mustn't meet. Delivan won't fight the way Preston does. He's liable to shoot Preston in the back—or hire one of his miserable gunmen to ambush Quent!"

Gorine raised startled brows, and then hastened after his own horse.

"So that," whispered the major to himself, "is how the wind blows!"

XV

DUE PROCESS OF LAW

A SICKLE of yellow moon cruised the Wyoming sky, shedding a fitful glow over the sagebrush flats where Wagonwheel City roared with the activity that always attended pay day.

Late that evening the Union Pacific paycar had pulled up on a siding, drawn by a snorting locomotive whose woodwork bore the broken shafts of Sioux arrows.

For hours after sundown, spikers and graders and tie cutters, cooks and rail layers and trestlemen—the vast legion of brawny workmen who were cogs in the mighty machinery of the railroad building—had passed in line through the paycar, drawing their wages.

Now that money was finding its way across bar counters, into dance hall tills, into the pockets of gamblers by way of faro and roulette and poker and chuckaluck.

Three men had died in gun smoke since sundown. There would be at least a dozen new graves on Cemetery Hill before another sunset, if tonight was an average pay day in the construction camp.

Quent Preston rode past Wagonwheel Springs

shortly before midnight. He had little fear of being recognized as the same cowboy who had escaped a lynch mob at this spot only a few days before. His face was more gaunt and hard-chiseled as a result of the suffering that had put the cruel shadows there, and his clothes were tattered and worn.

His ride out of the Sioux Bonnets had been a slow one, what with the ever-present threat of crossing trails again with the three straight-shooting raiders that had killed Weldon back in Tomahawk Pass. But he had seen no trace of the outlaws along the circuitous route he had chosen to the U. P. end-of-track town.

Somewhere in this mad beehive he would find Boone Delivan, smug and confident and immaculate. Whether Delivan maintained an office, or whether he owned one of the innumerable dwelling tents on the outskirts of the camp, Preston had no idea.

But there was no reason for haste. Showdown with Delivan could wait till the morrow. He doubted if the suave speculator mingled with the night life of end-of-track; his face had shown no evidence of all-night gambling or of whiskey bouts. Delivan depended on speed of wit and would be too shrewd a man to dull his brain with dissipation. Carousing was for the brawny railway laborers, not for a man of Boone Delivan's type.

Quent found a huge canvas barn resembling a circus tent across whose front was scribbled: "Shamrock Livery Stable. Horses Groomed & Grained, $5.00 per Day."

He turned Alamo over to a bearded hostler, who bit the tendered twenty-dollar gold piece and was gone into the labyrinth of stalls before the cowboy had counted his change and found a two-dollar shortage.

With a wry grin, Quent made his way out into the pedestrian traffic of the main street, intending to locate a hotel and get lodging for the night. Tomorrow promised to be a busy day, and one in which he would need rested nerves.

Out of the shadow of a narrow alley between the Union Pacific's field headquarters and a dingy saloon stepped a cadaverous-looking man on whose vest front gleamed a nickel-plated star.

A moment later, Preston found his path blocked by the peace officer, and his heart bounded within him as he recognized the bleary eyes and pinched features of Lige Morton, the city marshal whose hand had put a slipnoose over his throat at the intended lynching bee under the Wagonwheel Springs cottonwood tree.

"Preston, eh? You're under arrest, hombre. If you figgered you could murder Cy Trollen and then come back to brag about it, you're mist—"

Quent Preston shot out an arm to seize Morton's

wrist even as the scrawny marshal got a six-gun half out of leather. In the same movement the cowboy shoved Morton into the blotting shadows of the alley, pushing the marshal's back against the clapboard walls of the U. P. office.

"You ain't arrestin' nobody, tin star!" rasped the Texan, giving Morton's arm a wrench which caused him to drop his Colt .45 into the dirt. "I didn't come here looking for trouble and I don't aim to let you cook it up."

Morton opened his mouth to scream for help, but Preston's throttling fingers discouraged that idea.

Hauling back his left fist, the cowboy drove a hard punch to Morton's plowshare jaw, and the marshal sprawled in the darkness, shaking his head dazedly.

Then Preston stooped, found the lawman's gun in the dust underfoot and ejected the cartridges from the cylinder. He tossed the empty gun in Morton's general direction and then strode on down the board sidewalk. By the time the half-stunned marshal had recovered, Preston knew he would be lost in the teeming maze of Wagonwheel City.

A dozen yards away his eyes lighted on a canvas-roofed shack. Lamplight glowed through a square window facing the street and painted on the glass was a legend which caught the Texan's interest:

BAYARD'S LAND OFFICE
Ellis Bayard, Attorney
RIGHT-OF-WAY CLAIMS
ARE OUR SPECIALTY

Glancing through the window, Preston saw the bald-headed lawyer seated alone at his desk, working at a sheaf of papers spread out before him. The cowboy recalled that he had talked briefly to the corpulent lawyer on his previous visit to the camp.

"Mebbe this is where I can get the information I'm after."

Ellis Bayard answered the Texan's knock and had invited him inside before recognition made the fat attorney start.

". . . I hardly expected to see you back in town, Preston," stammered the lawyer, sliding a chair forward. "What brings you here this time of night?"

Quent twirled his Stetson on a forefinger and fished with his other hand in a buckskin pocket for cigarette makings.

"To talk business, I reckon. How much red tape is there to selling right of way to the U. P.?"

Bayard settled himself into his swivel chair, sweat dewing his face under the glare of a kerosene lamp overhead.

"Well . . . uh . . . that depends, Mr. Preston. Are you speaking of your homestead up in Tomahawk Pass?"

"That's right."

"But that is a hundred miles north of the railroad survey—"

Tersely, Quent Preston supplied the lawyer with the information given him that morning by Major John Gorine, the survey chief. Bayard's inward agitation became more pronounced as Preston went on.

"Uh—very interesting," answered the lawyer, when Preston had finished. "I suppose you have your homestead title papers?"

"I can get 'em. They're buried under the floor of my cabin—which same burned down last night."

Bayard fussed through the papers on his desk for a moment, as if hunting for something in particular. Then he rose.

"We must first make out an application to present to the Union Pacific officials," said the lawyer. "After your right of way is appraised we can complete the deal and get our money. My commission will be five percent of your net."

Bayard paused with his hand on the knob of a door leading to a back room.

"I keep my blank application forms out here," he said. "You wait here, Mr. Preston. I'll be back in a moment and explain the legalities to you in detail. You'll save time and expense by letting me handle this for you according to due process of law."

Bayard disappeared. The cowboy thought he heard another door open and close; then there was silence. He was beginning to regret having brought up the matter so late at night, after five minutes had elapsed. Then the rear door opened and Ellis Bayard stood on the threshold, his mutton chops glowing from the rear light of a lamp in his back room.

"We can work better in here away from the street noise," smirked the lawyer. "This business won't take long, Preston."

The cowboy got to his feet and walked through the doorway, squinting against the blinding light of a kerosene lamp.

Then his brain seemed to explode, as he was knocked down by a terrific blow from behind. As he rolled over on the earthen floor he groped instinctively for his guns. A man was bending over him with an upraised gun butt.

Quent was slipping off into an abyss of darkness. His last conscious sight was looking up into the venomous face of Boone Delivan. Then all faded into a black, terrible void.

XVI

FRAMED FOR MURDER

DELIVAN thrust his blood-smeared revolver into a holster under his armpit and withdrew his hand from beneath the lapel of his black frock coat.

Quent Preston lay motionless at the speculator's feet.

"Fast work, calling me over here," panted Delivan gratefully, his eyes on the pasty-faced lawyer. "It won't be hard to dispose of Preston's body before daylight—then we'll be set."

Bayard mopped a handkerchief over his shiny face and moisture-dripping double chins. He inquired shakily:

"Is he dead?"

Delivan stooped to inspect the ghastly welt on the Texan's head. The clubbing gun butt had split the scalp to expose raw bone beneath.

"No. But that can be managed without noise—or should we gag him and tie him up, and force him to sign over title papers to Tomahawk Pass when he comes to?"

The lawyer took down a whiskey bottle from a shelf and swigged a stiff drink to bolster his shattered nerves. Bayard was not used to violence. The occasional shooting scrapes he had

106

seen on the main street had left him with a nauseated feeling.

This was the first time Bayard had ever actually witnessed the ruthless side of Boone Delivan's nature. He had guessed, and correctly, that the smooth-mannered renegade was out here on the frontier because of some crime he had committed in the East. But heretofore, Ellis Bayard's unscrupulous talents had been linked to Delivan only as the speculator's legal front.

"No . . . no. Get him out of my place," pleaded the lawyer. "I can't have a body found in here. We . . . we can forge his signature easily enough."

The lawyer brightened as he remembered something.

"We've got this Tomahawk Pass deal in the bag. Preston just got through telling me his government deed to the ranch homestead is buried under the floor of his cabin. It shouldn't take long to dig it up—"

Both men started violently as they heard boots slogging up the front steps of Bayard's office, from the main street.

They knew it was impossible that any passerby could have seen Delivan slug the cowboy here in the back room, for Bayard had closed the door after Preston's entrance.

Delivan stooped to peer through the keyhole in time to see the front door kicked open without the formality of a knock. Framed on the top doorstep was the disheveled figure of Lige Morton, the city marshal.

Indistinct against the backdrop of the night were two burly men in United States army uniforms.

"Preston come in here after he beat me up!" screamed the marshal, pointing a bony finger into the lawyer's office. "I seen him with my own eyes, talkin' to Bayard—just before I got you! Come on!"

Both of the soldiers bore the arm badges of military police, whose duties consisted of patrolling the construction camp of nights and keeping law and order. Their authority was supreme, Lige Morton being a mere figurehead hired by the saloons to eject troublesome customers.

"We'll try the back room, Morton!" clipped one of the military policemen. "There's a light back there—"

Boone Delivan stooped and jerked one of Quent Preston's .45 Colts from its holster. Aiming through the keyhole, he sent a bullet smashing through the thin-paneled partition.

Out in the front office, Lige Morton gagged on a scream of agony and clawed at a spouting bullet hole in his stomach. Then, twisting sideways as his knees buckled, the marshal pitched backward against the very legs of the startled soldiers.

With incredibly fast movements, Delivan

inserted the smoking six-gun in Preston's limp hand. Then, rising through a curtain of billowing gun fumes, he dug iron-muscled fingers into Bayard's trembling arm and hissed out:

"Tell those army men that Preston shot Morton, understand? Then you knocked Preston out with that whiskey bottle!"

Before Ellis Bayard could draw in a gasping breath, Boone Delivan had stepped noiselessly to a side window, straddled the sill, and dropped into the blackness of the night.

From the front room came a harsh command:

"Open up and come out with your hands up!"

Bayard gulped hard. He stared down at the whiskey bottle, transferred his pudgy hand to the neck of the bottle. Then, stumbling forward, the corpulent lawyer shoved open the partition door and faced the grim military police.

Both soldiers stood wide-legged behind Morton's twitching corpse, their heavy-bore army pistols trained at Bayard.

"Hell's bells!" ejaculated one of the policemen, whom Bayard recognized as a Corporal Tracy. "Who'd ever thought that fat shyster had the guts to commit a murder!"

Bayard made a sickly grin and stood aside to reveal Quent Preston's prostrate body to the startled soldiers.

"It wasn't me who . . . who shot, corporal," stammered the lawyer in a sick voice. "This

Preston fellow did it—without warning—when Morton came into my front office Preston pulled a gun and shot—then I knocked him out with this bottle—"

Corporal Tracy holstered his pistol and stepped over Morton's body on his way to the partition door.

"I'll be damned!" breathed the soldier admiringly. "So you belted him on the noggin with that bottle, eh? Good work!"

The lawyer nodded eagerly, cheeks ballooning with relief as he saw that Delivan's trumped-up explanation of the killing had passed muster with the hard-eyed military police.

"That's right, corporal. Oh—this is awful—had no idea— We were talking over a business deal —had come back here to get a drink of bourbon —then this happened—"

Bayard glanced over at Morton's corpse. His shudder at sight of the marshal's blood, clotting in a sticky puddle on the floor, was so genuine it brought a grin of sympathy to the corporal.

"Take it easy, Bayard. We'll handle this gunman— Who is he, you know?"

"His name's Preston. I think—he's the same man who killed that Trollen fellow over by the waterhole several days ago."

The two soldiers entered the back room and knelt beside Preston's limp form. One of them removed the smoking Colt from the cowboy's

110

hand and nodded significantly. The other was examining the splinter-collared puncture in the flimsy partition, where the fatal slug had sped on its way to Morton's body.

"Wonder what Preston had against Morton?" mused Corporal Tracy curiously. "He came running up to us just as Sergeant Kelly here and me were coming out of the Red Tent Saloon. Said he'd been disarmed and beat up by Preston a few minutes ago."

"It's a damned shame we didn't surround the building," put in Sergeant Kelly, "otherwise Morton would be alive now."

Bayard took another drink from the amber bottle in his hands, the whiskey leaking down his pink-shaven chins.

"Preston was a desperate character—wanted for killing a sheriff down in Texas," fabricated the lawyer, his tongue getting more fluent now that the alcohol was in his blood. "I shouldn't have let him in my office in the first place."

The two army policemen lifted Preston by the armpits, hoisting the six-foot-four cowboy to his feet with difficulty.

"Colonel Sires is holding a court-martial tomorrow morning for some other murderers," said Tracy. "They'll see to it that Preston doesn't pull off another killing. You better be on hand at the court-martial, Bayard, to help testify."

The paunchy lawyer followed the officers to

111

the front door, rubbing flabby palms together with satisfaction.

"Of course, corporal, of course. I will be on hand."

Curious spectators halted out in the street as they saw the burly soldiers emerge from Bayard's Land Office with Quent Preston's inert bulk hanging limply in the grasps of his captors.

"We'll send men back for Morton's body as quick as we get this desperado locked up in the jail car," said Tracy. "Don't let anybody in to disturb the body."

Bayard bowed jerkily, resembling a toadlike Japanese god in the doorway. "I shan't let any-one in," he reassured them.

XVII

GORINE DECLARES HIMSELF

THE largest and most pretentious structure in Wagonwheel City was the End-of-Track Hotel.

Its mammoth spread of canvas roofs covered an area a city block square, and was divided off into dozens of rooms and a maze of corridors by means of flimsy portable partitions.

Ten dollars per night was the fee for the dubious privilege of resting on cheap army cots with one blanket and no conveniences other than a packing-case dresser, a pitcher of water, and a tallow candle. Yet the End-of-Track register was always full.

A fifty-by-hundred-foot lobby flanked the main street. Its earthen floor was copiously sawdusted. A bar with an imported mahogany counter and huge back-bar mirror occupied a prominent corner. From sundown until three o'clock every morning the lobby was ablaze with the lights of a score of suspended lamps.

At this hostelry gathered the richer classes. Union Pacific stockholders, professional gamblers, army officers, silk-hatted capitalists out from New York or Philadelphia or St. Louis to visit the turbulent scenes at end-of-track.

It was natural that Boone Delivan should choose to make his living quarters in the End-of-Track Hotel. He maintained a "suite" of rooms as pretentious as those occupied by General Dodge on his inspection tours.

After Delivan had made his hasty and secret departure from the dangerous locality of Bayard's back room, he crossed the main street at an unhurried gait, attracting no attention whatsoever.

He was sure no one had noticed Ellis Bayard coming through the hotel lobby to summon him over to the Land Office less than five minutes before. Delivan had always been careful not to cultivate acquaintances. Therefore his comings and goings were always unnoticed in the hubbub of the town's restless life.

A consummate sense of victory filled Delivan's being as he headed for a luxurious leather-cushioned settee facing the hotel's bat-wing doors, and seated himself there.

As Bayard had said, the Tomahawk Pass right-of-way deal was in the bag. With Preston once out of the way a tidy fortune would drop into Delivan's lap, with proper maneuvering of forged documents and bribe money paid to the proper Union Pacific grafters.

Taking an expensive Cuban cheroot from his waistcoat pocket, Delivan lighted up, puffed luxuriously, and unfolded a copy of a Baltimore paper which devoted several front-page columns to the progress of the Union Pacific railroad, fast reaching its terminus in Utah.

The paper made much of the Sioux attacks which had harried the line, describing how work trains were derailed and bridges destroyed and rails torn up by the hostile Indian war parties.

The Central Pacific, by contrast, was hindered only by the heat of the arid desert terrain it was spanning through from California.

Delivan was engrossed in the newspaper when he heard his name called out sharply in the din of the lobby.

Without betraying his inward jump of alarm, the speculator lowered his paper and glanced up. Major John Gorine and Helen were standing before him, hats in hand, their clothes moist with horse sweat and dusty with the alkali of a long trail.

"Well! This *is* a surprise!" greeted Delivan heartily, with his usual flashing smile as he stood up and bowed to Helen. "What brings you folks to Wagonwheel City this time of night?"

Delivan's voice trailed off as he saw the fire in Helen's eyes, her locked mouth and clenched fists. Major Gorine was glowering at him and his greeting had been hostile.

"I beg your pardon," apologized the speculator, standing aside to point to the settee. "Won't you sit down?"

Major Gorine stepped forward, eyes blazing into Delivan's.

"No, thank you. Thank God, we aren't too late—but we sighted a big Sioux camp on the way down, and had to circle twenty miles out of the way."

Delivan's brow gathered into worried lines. Never had the Gorines spoken in such truculent accents. Yet it was evident that the father and daughter had just arrived. That being the case, it was doubtful that they knew of Preston's arrest.

"What's wrong?" inquired Delivan gravely. "Why . . . why do you look at me this way, Helen?"

Major Gorine's fiery gaze silenced Delivan.

"You might as well have the blunt truth, Boone. Your paid killer, Weldon, has stripped off your sheep's clothing. Helen and I know exactly the stripe of cur you are."

Delivan exhaled a long breath of cheroot smoke. His masklike face gave no hint of his mental turmoil.

The three surviving members of his raiding gang to Tomahawk Pass had reported at Wagonwheel Springs at dusk, telling Delivan of the destruction of Preston's range and the heavy toll which the Texas cowboy had taken of the other members of the raiding gang.

They had reported, likewise, the death of Weldon on the trail out of Tomahawk Pass that

116

morning. But Delivan had not dreamed that Weldon had turned traitor and betrayed him.

"There must be some mistake," insisted the speculator blandly. "I have never heard of a gentleman named Weldon, much less hired him. It wounds me deeply to think that Helen could mistrust—"

Major Gorine moved between his daughter and the nonchalant speculator, as if to protect her from Delivan's tolerant gaze.

"Boone, we rode here to warn you to get out of town. To get as far from here as you can. Preston's looking for you. He'll kill you on sight."

Delivan flicked ash from his cigar with a manicured nail.

"If you both hate me—why do you ride fifty miles to warn me to beware of this desperado?"

"Because," flared the railway surveyor hotly, "we don't want your blood on Preston's hands. We want you to get out, damn you—take your filthy money and get out before Preston sends you to the cemetery where you belong!"

Delivan bowed mockingly, his face betraying no concern.

"All this is most interesting. I—"

Delivan broke off as he caught sight of Ellis Bayard shouldering through the batwing doors of the hotel lobby and heading in his direction, face purple with excitement.

"Boone! Boone!" cried the lawyer, lumbering up to the speculator's side. "Preston—oh, excuse me. Miss Gorine—Major—"

Delivan's eyes flashed a warning to the agitated lawyer.

"What's all the excitement, Mr. Bayard?"

The lawyer rolled his eyes, gulped, looked from Delivan to the Gorines, and then panted heavily:

"An awful thing just happened over in my office, Boone. Quent Preston—that Texan you saved from hanging, remember? He came into my office to get me to handle a right-of-way deal for him. And—and the town marshal came in, Lige Morton. And in cold blood, Preston shot Morton dead!"

Major Gorine's face went chalky white. He groped out an arm to draw Helen closer to him.

"Apparently your friend Mr. Preston is going to shoot up the whole town until he finds me," said Delivan sarcastically. "What became of Mr. Preston, Bayard? Did he escape?"

Bayard swabbed his face with a moist handkerchief.

"No, thank heavens. The killer got his just deserts. Two army policemen were with Morton at the time. I . . . I knocked out Preston with a bottle. They took him to jail. He's to be court-martialed in the morning."

Helen Gorine and her engineer father stared at each other in mutual horror. Then Major Gorine drew back his shoulders and bit out defiantly:

"I'll be at that court-martial tomorrow, Delivan. After I've finished my testimony in Preston's behalf, you'll wish you'd gotten out of Wagonwheel City!"

With which words, Gorine turned on his heel and left the hotel, Helen at his side.

After the bat-wing doors had flapped shut on their departure, Delivan said to Bayard without moving his eyes from the door:

"There'll be hell to pay if Gorine testifies, Bayard. He knows enough to hang the two of us."

Bayard's flabby face turned to the color of banana meat.

"You can't—drag me into this!" whined the lawyer. "I . . . I've done your dirty work so far as doctoring papers is concerned. But . . . I didn't contract . . . to get mixed up with murder, Boone!"

Delivan flicked his cheroot stub to the floor and cut off Bayard with an angry oath, his eyes still gimleting into space.

"Keep your blabbing mouth shut, Bayard. You won't be mixed up in this. I'll make sure Major Gorine doesn't spill the beans at Preston's hearing tomorrow morning!"

XVIII

COURT-MARTIAL

IT was still dark when Quent Preston recovered consciousness to find himself stretched on a cold wooden floor.

He sat up, groping both hands to his temples. The entire back of his skull seemed to be splitting open, stabbing darts of pain hammering his brain at each throb of his heart.

His fingers came away sticky from an egg-sized welt above his left temple. The touch of his hand brought on nausea and faintness, and he sagged back on the splintery floor, moaning.

Gradually as his senses cleared, Preston became conscious of vague sounds. The raucous yells of men, mingled with the occasional high-pitched laughter of women.

Somewhere a wolf bayed at the stars on a distant ridge. It was the only familiar sound that reached Quent's ears.

After an eternity of lying on the hard floor, Preston stirred himself and sat up. The pain was undiminished in his head, but memory began to return as he cudgeled his brain to figure out his present predicament.

"Let's see—I was going into that lawyer's

back room—then I must have been slugged—Delivan—*Delivan!*"

The name hissed from his lips like something unclean to be spat from his mouth. The name brought back, in a hideous rush, all the hate and revenge lust that had smoldered there during his ride out of the Sioux Bonnets the afternoon before.

Groping in the pocket of his buckskin shirt, the cowboy found matches. He struck one and peered about, eyes widening with puzzlement at the strangeness of his surroundings.

He was sitting on the floor of a cubicle six feet square. Two of the walls were of heavy wooden timbers, painted maroon. The other two walls were formed of thick iron latticework, rusty in patches. A tremendous iron lock marked a door.

Shakily, the Texan got to his feet, and his head came level with a small barred window on his left. A night breeze blew out the match in his fingers, and he stood there, hanging to one iron-latticed wall for support.

Peering out, he caught sight of the glowing, lamp-lighted tents of Wagonwheel City, like ghostly blobs in the night. The prison in which he found himself seemed to be elevated a dozen feet above the sagebrush flats on which the construction camp was built.

A shifting wind brought a hodgepodge of sound from the town: tin-panny music from an

121

off-key piano; bottles rattling on saloon shelves; the shouts of a barker outside a dance hall; the yammer of dogs.

"Wonder where in hell I am, and how I got here?"

Preston struck another match and set fire to a crumpled newspaper on the floor. The flames threw out a lemon-yellow glare, and by the guttering light Preston discovered that he was inside a railroad car.

He recognized the curved, varnished ceiling with its roof ventilators and hanging kerosene lamps; sliding doors a dozen feet from his cell. A man slept, curled up like a dog, in an adjoining cage. Over by the car door a sentry in army uniform roused out of a doze and jumped up with an oath.

"What you tryin' to do, man—burn down the car? Stomp out that paper!"

"What am I doing in here?" demanded Preston as the guard peered through the latticework at him.

"You're in the army hoosegow, feller. Put out that fire!"

"In jail? What in hell for?"

The sentry grunted sarcastically. "For killin' the town marshal, that's all. Or have you forgotten?"

A cold shock went through Preston. Lige Morton dead? Quent remembered striking the scrawny marshal, but it had not even been a knock-out blow. It seemed impossible that Morton could have died as a result of his punch.

The flaming newspaper turned to curling, pink-edged ashes in the corner of his cell. A wet ooze filmed Preston's face.

"I didn't kill Morton," he protested in a low voice. "I've been framed somehow. Boone Delivan and—"

"Save your arguments for the court-martial, feller. It's four A.M. now. You'll be facin' a military judge at eight, so calm down and don't wake up these other poor devils."

The sentry returned to his post by the door of the wheeled jailhouse and resumed his snoring.

Preston propped himself in a seated position in the corner, his heart a dull weight in his chest, and tried to think things out. Exhaustion brought on merciful drowsiness, and Preston slept.

Sunshine was streaming into the jail car and a rough hand was shaking him when Preston next opened his eyes.

The pain in his head had increased to a dull, steady ache. He looked up to see three soldiers standing in the doorway of his cell. One of them had just finished locking a pair of huge iron fetters about his wrists, the cold contact of the metal sending goose pimples up his arms.

"All right, Preston. You've got just time to gulp

123

down some coffee before we rustle you over to headquarters. Get up."

Preston blinked, shaking his head to clear it. Numbly he accepted a tin cup full of black coffee that a soldier thrust in his manacled hands. He gulped the unsweetened liquid and felt energy return as the strong coffee reached his stomach.

Through the barred window he saw Wagonwheel City. Next to the jail car were the gleaming tracks of the main line of the U. P. R., newly hewn ties turning yellow in the sun.

"Hurry along, Preston. You're already due at the court-martial. Hustle up."

Someone took the half-emptied coffee cup from his hands. The cowboy ducked mechanically to avoid hitting his head on the six-foot lintel of the cell door.

Rough hands escorted him out past rows of identical cells and down an iron step to the ground. The hot sunshine felt good, and he filled his lungs with the crisp morning air.

He was marched at a rapid gait across a parade ground where a troop of crack horsemen were drilling, the American flag and regimental pennants whipping in the breeze.

Two minutes later he and his escorts followed a saber-clanking lieutenant up to a frame shack which flew a flag marked: "HEADQUARTERS BATTALION K, U. S. CAVALRY. LT. COLONEL FRANK SIRES, COMMANDING."

The cowboy was escorted indoors to find himself in a room filled with medal-bedecked officers belonging to the high command of the Wagonwheel City battalion of troops.

A stern-visaged man whom he heard addressed as Colonel Sires was seated at a polished desk, grim as a judge in a courtroom. An air of tension had filled the house at his entrance, and Quent felt the hairs on his neck prickle as he met a battery of staring eyes from all sides.

"You are Quent Preston?" demanded Colonel Sires, consulting some papers before him. "Very well—take the oath."

Preston mumbled as he was sworn in. He caught sight of Ellis Bayard, the pot-bellied land-office lawyer, seated among the spectators.

"You are being court-martialed this morning, Preston, on three serious charges," intoned the army commander. "The immediate charge, which caused your arrest last night, was the murder of Lige Morton, resident marshal."

Before Preston could snarl out a denial, Sires went on:

"There is also the matter of the death of one Linn DePerren on Tuesday last, at Major John Gorine's survey camp in Tomahawk Pass. There has also come to our attention the fact that you were responsible for the death of one Cyrus

Trollen on the ninth of this month, here in Wagonwheel City."

Preston's heart sank in despair before the rapid-fire recital of charges against him. In his befuddled mental condition he had difficulty in remembering the names of DePerren and Trollen, let alone the circumstances linking him to their deaths.

"We will take up the matter of Lige Morton's death first, Preston. Do you plead guilty or not guilty to this charge?"

Preston shook his head dumbly.

"I didn't kill Morton. The last I remember, Boone Del—"

Colonel Sires slapped his desk with a gavel that resounded like a pistol shot.

"Very well—the prisoner pleads not guilty. We have three eyewitnesses to this killing: Attorney Ellis Bayard and Military Patrolmen Jack Tracy and George Kelly. Call Mr. Bayard to the stand, if you please, adjutant."

The hour that followed was a nightmare. Quent Preston's ears recorded the damning testimony of Ellis Bayard and the two army policemen who had taken him to jail, but the words meant nothing, only confused his already befuddled brain.

When the case concerning Lige Morton was disposed of, the matter of Linn DePerren's death was next brought up.

Staring at the floor, Preston listened to Colonel Sires read a letter which was signed by Major John Gorine.

"Major Gorine seems to be in some doubt as to whether or not Preston shot in self-defense in this DePerren case," said Colonel Sires. "However, we shall not call Major Gorine in from his survey camp inasmuch as Preston has already been found guilty of the murder of Lige Morton last night."

Preston felt a tense flutter go around the room as Colonel Sires stood up, his eyes fixed on the cowboy's face.

"We will not tangle this court-martial with needless red tape regarding the two other murder charges against you, Preston. Before sentence is passed, have you anything to say?"

The Texan shook himself out of his torpor and pressed iron-shackled hands to his aching temples.

He was conscious of the fact that disaster was engulfing him, yet he seemed powerless to clear his mind enough to protest his innocence.

"I'm not guilty—Colonel Sires," he finally gritted out. "If you could talk to Major Gorine, he could tell you—who's at the bottom of 'em. But I—"

Preston's voice trailed off into a whisper. His head was throbbing like a trip hammer and the room swam dizzily before his eyes.

As if from a great distance, he heard Colonel Sires' voice tolling like a knell of doom:

"—this court-martial having found you guilty as charged of the murder of Marshal Lige Morton, you will face a military firing squad tomorrow at sunrise. Court is adjourned!"

XIX

DEATH BY STABBING

HELEN GORINE spent a sleepless night in her ill-ventilated room in the Irish Rose Hotel, a modest hostelry situated on the side street. She and her father selected this small hotel on their infrequent trips to end-of-track because it was away from the noisy bedlam of the main street.

Dawn found the girl washing her face and hands in a cracked bowl of icy water. Her toilet finished, she rapped lightly on the clapboard partition which adjoined her father's room, but got no response.

"It's early—I might as well let him sleep," she decided. "The court-martial isn't until eight."

Because it would be at least two hours before it would be necessary for her father to arise, Helen decided to take a walk and get some fresh air. Two hours of being cooped up in the tiny hotel room would do her frayed nerves no good.

She found Wagonwheel City quieter than she had ever seen it. Haggard-faced swampers were cleaning out saloons. Three times during her walk toward the springs, Helen had to avert her gaze from the grim spectacle of men carrying limp, unshrouded corpses toward the field of unmarked graves on the hillside.

129

The army of U. P. workmen—spikers, track gaugers, rail layers, tie-setters, gang foremen— were scrambling aboard the work train which would take them out to end-of-track, now fifteen miles west of Wagonwheel City.

Accompanying the work train was a long string of flatcars laden to capacity with blue-uniformed soldiers and their mounts, as protection against the ever-increasing threat of Indian attack.

The invisible menace of the Sioux had a sobering effect on everyone. Scouts had reported that the Indians were massing in the broken hills northwest of Wagonwheel City. The Indians might attack the railroad crews in overwhelming numbers at any moment.

At seven o'clock the girl turned back to the Irish Rose Hotel. There would be ample time to rouse her father, have breakfast in a restaurant— where fresh eggs cost fifty cents each, and a cup of stale coffee brought two bits—and get over to the army barracks in time to attend Quent Preston's hearing.

She paused at the door of her father's room and called his name. Receiving no reply, Helen knocked, softly at first, then louder as she got no response.

"I never knew him to sleep so soundly, poor dear," she muttered. "The trip must have tired him out and—"

She noted, with surprise, that the key was

projecting from the door lock. This was unusual, for Major Gorine had always cautioned her to lock her room as protection against night prowlers and drunks, and he had always observed the same practice himself.

Swinging the door open, Helen's mouth was framed to call out a cheery greeting to awaken Major Gorine.

Instead, she caught a hand to her throat and gave a piercing scream which resounded in echo down the flimsy-walled hallway.

"Daddy—daddy—"

Major John Gorine lay on the bedroom cot, heavy-lidded eyes staring at the canvas ceiling. Both his hands were above the blankets, frozen there in the act of clutching the haft of a bowie knife which had been plunged to the hilt into the old surveyor's heart.

When the initial shock had passed, Helen collected herself with a supreme effort. For twenty of her twenty-four years her father had been her only living kin. She loved him with the passionate ardor that an only child can feel toward a kindly and understanding parent.

But her years on the wild frontier had given Helen a strength of will over her emotions which a city-bred woman of her own age would not have possessed. Therefore, she quelled the sob which tore at her throat and forced herself to cross the room and touch Major Gorine's forehead.

It was cold. Undoubtedly he had been dead many hours. Death from an unknown assassin's blade had probably occurred shortly after he and his daughter had retired.

Her scream summoned the owner of the hotel, a black-whiskered Irishman named Hennessy. With him were two wide-eyed charwomen, who blanched as they saw the tragic picture of Helen staring in mute horror at the corpse on the bed.

"Domn an' begorra!" cried Hennessy, entering the room and crossing himself. "Sure and what an evil reppitation my hoos will get if the town hears a mon loike Major Gorine was murthered as he shlept under my roof—"

Helen tore herself away, faced the opposite wall.

"Some robber, thinkin' he had money, don't yez believe, Moike?" asked one of the charwomen, covering the dead man's head with a quilt. " 'Tis a baistly shame, thot it is—"

Helen took a deep breath, held her voice in control as she said: "No—no. It was deliberate murder. Someone wanted him dead. How—could anyone find out—this was daddy's room?"

The baldheaded old Irishman shrugged, avoiding the girl's pain-brightened eyes.

"Begorra, miss, it would be aisy-like to find oot where the major shlept, by lookin' in the register in the lobby—"

132

• • •

The pain of the ensuing hours was mercifully dimmed in the girl's memory by its sheer horror. Roughly sympathetic, the charwomen superintended the ghastly business of transferring the major's corpse to a tent on the east side of town where it would be prepared for burial by a renegade undertaker who was doing a flourishing business in the construction town.

Only then, when she could no longer be at her dead father's side, did the crushing realization that she was utterly alone in the world strike Helen Gorine's heart.

Leaving the undertaker's tent, she caught sight of a clock in a restaurant window. The hands pointed to 9:30. The shock of seeing how the morning had sped wrenched Helen out of her stupor of grief.

"Quent Preston—his trial was to be at eight—"

Oblivious to the leers of men on the street, Helen fled across town to the army barracks and was directed by a pacing sentry to the headquarters building.

There she learned that the morning's court-martial session had been over for a half-hour, and that four men had been condemned to meet death before a firing squad for sundry crimes.

"Was—one of the condemned—named Preston?" She braced herself so as not to flinch at the soldier's answer.

"Yes, ma'am," replied the aide de camp. "A cowboy named Preston shot up the town last night, killed the marshal."

"Where . . . where is he now?"

The aide de camp pointed across the drill ground toward a grim-looking red box car with barred windows on the railroad siding.

"That car with U. P. R. 1367 on its side, ma'am. Uh—you don't happen to be Mr. Preston's wife, by any cha—"

But she was gone, running across the deserted drill ground as fast as her legs could carry her. The car door was open, for ventilating purposes, and Helen Gorine was inside the car before a startled sentry thew down a book he had been reading and jumped up from his chair.

"Hey—you can't come in here—"

But Helen was already on her way to the cell at the end of the car, where she saw Quent Preston seated on a stool, staring moodily at the floor. He looked up as she reached the door, and a glad smile wiped off the blank despair in his face.

"Helen Gorine!" cried the Texan. "Did your—your father come with you from the Sioux Bonnets? He can get me out of this mess—"

Only then, as her hands grasped Preston's through the bars, did Helen Gorine break down. When her sobs had diminished, she choked out:

"Oh, Quent . . . my daddy . . . was going to testify for you at the court-martial . . . but—"

"Shucks, miss," gruffed Preston as she choked into silence. "I don't reckon the major could have helped me much. Boone Delivan had enough killings chalked up to me to hang a dozen men, and he covered his tracks like a lobo wolf."

She lifted tear-streaming eyes to his.

"But daddy . . . was stabbed to death . . . last night. I'm positive . . . it was to prevent him . . . from testifying against Boone Delivan!"

The heavy hand of the guard laid on the girl's shoulder before Preston could recover from the shock of her news.

"No visitors allowed to see the condemned men, miss. You better leave. It's agin' regulations to be in here—"

Quent's hands clung to the girl's, but the sentry pulled her toward the car door.

She flung a last glance over her shoulder at Quent Preston's ash-pale face behind the latticework, and then felt herself lifted unceremoniously to the ground.

"Listen," she said to the guard, as he started to apologize. "Tell me . . . the execution . . . where . . . when—"

The sentry dug his hobnailed boot into the dust.

"Usually the firing squads—do it in camp," he said awkwardly. "But we ain't got a fenced-off place here in Wagonwheel City, so the Old Man's give orders to hook a locomotive onto this jail car and drag it west of town about five miles."

"Where?" she queried, once more in control of her emotions.

"Well, out where the railroad cuts through Bitterroot Ridge, the orders read. But—ma'am—you ain't figuring to go out and witness—the shootin'tomorrow, are you?"

Helen Gorine turned away and walked down the sidetrack until she was directly under the tiny barred window of Preston's cell.

"Quent!" she called, and saw the cowboy's face framed in the window overhead. "Quent—your horse—where is he stabled?"

Preston gulped hard and forced a grin.

"I'm glad you asked, Miss Gorine. Alamo's over in the Shamrock livery barn. I sort of wish—after tomorrow—you'd take care of old Alamo, miss. You love horseflesh, and he sorta—"

Helen moved away from the car as she saw the sentry coming in her direction, head cocked suspiciously.

"*Hasta la vista,* Quent!" she called enigmatically. "Isn't that how they say it down in Texas?"

Quent Preston watched her lithe figure vanish into the city of tents.

Adios, he told himself bitterly, would have been a more appropriate word for Helen to have used.

136

XX

DEATH AT SUNRISE

THE black, foreboding hour just before dawn found Wagonwheel asleep the following day. Swampers had emptied barrooms of the last drunk, sending them lurching on their way to gutters or their respective tents. Gambling-house wheels were idle after all-night roulette sessions.

Still a few minutes remained before the brassy notes of a bugle would rouse both the sleeping masses of railroad workers and their escorts, the United States troops.

Out on the siding which flanked the main line of the Union Pacific, a locomotive was panting out a volcano of smoke as the fireman stoked its grates with cordwood and the engineer eyed the dials registering his head of steam.

The locomotive was connected to the red jail car. Coupled behind the jailcar was a flatcar with an inclined ramp sloping up from the ground.

Quent Preston had roused from sleep a half-hour before the puffing, stealthy approach of the locomotive, and its jarring connection with the wheeled jail's coupling rods.

He had spent his last night on earth sleeping on the cold floorboards with only a single army blanket over him. What had awakened him was the panicked screams of two of the soldiers who had been sentenced to die that morning.

They were beating their cell bars in the maniacal fashion of doomed men afraid of eternity. They were staring out of barred windows, watching the Wyoming horizon to eastward as the stars were gradually banished before the advent of a rose-gray sunrise.

"Their damned shooting squad will be drawing a bead on us when that sun shows up!" sobbed one of the hysterical soldiers. "Why couldn't they have shot us yesterday—after court-martial—instead of doing everything according to damned rules and regulations—torturin' us!"

Preston rolled himself a smoke. Fear had not laid its icy clutches on the Texan's heart, though the firing squad was less than an hour away now. He had long since steeled himself to face his finish with jaw outthrust in defiance.

But a consuming sense of injustice kept his brow feverish. He wondered if Boone Delivan, who somehow had authored this fiendish travesty on justice, would be out there at Bitterroot Ridge to witness their execution.

Delivan had covered his tracks far too well ever to be apprehended, Preston knew.

The stabbing of Major John Gorine lay like a heavy weight on Preston's heart. Indirectly, Gorine's death had been due to him, Preston. Like Helen, Preston had no doubts as to the motive back of the survey chief's murder. Boone Delivan had had to silence Major Gorine, come what may—

Preston had kept his face glued to the cell window all the previous day in hope of catching one more glimpse of Helen, possibly mounted astride Alamo, his claybank pony. But it had been a fruitless vigil.

"The firing squad's comin' across the parade grounds, men!" announced the third of the trio of condemned soldiers, who, like Preston, was awaiting his end with stony indifference. "Colonel Sires is leading 'em out here."

Preston could not see the twelve horsemen whom Colonel Sires had selected, probably by lot, to be executioners today. But he heard the clatter of steel-shod hoofs as the horses were ridden up the sloping wooden runway onto the flatcar.

Then Preston saw Colonel Sires walk past his side of the jailcar, indistinct in the cold gray light, and mount into the engine cab.

"I guess we're ready, engineer," came the army commander's tired voice. "Let's get this nasty business over with."

Without clang of bell or blast of whistle, the death-bound train got in motion. Drive wheels clattered over frogs at the main-line switch; Wagonwheel City glided past in the semidarkness.

Indistinctly, Preston saw the dark blot of the

cottonwood trees overhanging Wagonwheel Springs. He tried to forget the time he and his father had camped there, on their way to Tomahawk Pass.

The train gathered speed, the snorting of its exhaust thrown back in taunting echoes of farewell by the logged-off hillside to the north, the hillside from whose summit the Prestons had first glimpsed the construction camp.

Sagebrush and dwarf piñons swam past in an ever-increasing blur as the locomotive gathered speed. A curve in the tracks shut Wagonwheel City from view and gave Preston a glimpse of the dozen rifle-armed cavalrymen who were huddled with their horses on the flatcar behind.

Smoke and cinders beat through his cell window. The rattle of trucks over rail joints helped muffle the laments of the two doomed men, Bates and Seiden.

Preston grinned wryly at the soldier named Leacock as he passed tobacco and papers through the adjoining bars.

"They don't do things up brown in the army out here at the edge of nowhere, do they?" commented Leacock. "We didn't even get a breakfast into our bellies, they're so anxious to get us lined up before that shootin' squad."

Preston drew at his own cigarette and kept his face framed in the barred window. The biting air was clean and cold and good in his nostrils, and he wanted to fill his lungs to the utmost with the beloved fragrance of sage and wild rose. He wondered if heaven, wherever that was, could be half so fair as these frontier open spaces.

A gray light was revealing the distant snow-covered Sioux Bonnets. A milepost scampered past. Two of them. A third—

Bitterroot Ridge was in sight now. The big yellow shale cut banks would be the backstop for the executioners' bullets. Colonel Sires would hurry the grim ordeal, for the death train had to get back to the Wagonwheel siding in time to clear the tracks for the troop train and work trains which would be going out to end-of-track shortly after daybreak.

The clamoring of the condemned men increased as the locomotive throttle was shut off and the train began coasting, losing speed.

The eastern horizon was aflame now; five more minutes would see the sun bursting in all its glory over the Wyoming terrain. That dawning sun would usher four souls into eternity.

The locomotive gave a short whistle to warn the cavalrymen on the flatcar to brace themselves for a stop. Two hundred yards ahead loomed the yellowish V of Bitterroot Ridge cut.

Brakes squealed on drive wheels, and with a jangle of iron couplings, the train came to a stop that was followed by a fatigued sigh of steam from the engine's cylinder cocks.

Preston saw the wooden gangplank shoved out again—and then the twelve uniformed troopers led their mounts down the cleated incline. After the death train had returned to Wagonwheel City, these soldiers would later mount the westward-bound troop train.

The jailcar door opened, flooding the gloomy interior with rose-tinted light. Bates and Seiden stiffened in their cages as Colonel Sires swung up from the ground. Leacock and Preston drew at their cigarettes in seeming indifference.

"The executions will be singly," clipped the army commander to the two sentries inside the car. "We will take the prisoners in the following order: Seiden, Leacock, Bates, Preston."

The mounted firing squad hobbled their ponies and lined up facing the slope of the cut. The sentries unlocked Seiden's cell and dragged the screaming soldier out to the shale bank.

Two minutes later, as the sun peeped its golden rim over the eastern hills, a sharp rattle of musketry rang out over the empty prairie.

When Quent's eyes were once more drawn toward the embankment a hundred yards away, it was to see gun smoke dissolving in the crisp air and a huddled figure at the base of the slope.

In ghastly succession, Leacock and Bates followed, the former flicking his cigarette butt aside and reminding Preston to join him with a glass of the devil's brew in hell.

Left alone with a single guard inside the jailcar, Quent Preston tried to settle his taut nerves by looking out the window toward the west, in the hopes that his beloved Tomahawk Pass would be his last sight on earth. But the intervening shoulder of Bitterroot Ridge cut off even that slight comfort.

Then, even as the shot rang out which sent the cringing Bates into eternity, Quent Preston caught sight of a lone figure emerging from a thicket of wild aspen near the U. P. right of way.

Sunlight flashed on the polished barrel of a rifle in the figure's grasp. The oncomer was headed for the cab of the locomotive, unnoticed by the firing squad in the distance.

Quent Preston's jaw dropped on an oath as he saw wind-blown chestnut hair fluttering back from a hard-set resolute face.

It was Helen Gorine!

XXI

SPURRING THE IRON HORSE

WITH masculine stride the girl walked toward the red-painted cab of the locomotive. The engineer and fireman were pretending to be busy with gauges and firebox, to avoid looking out to where three bodies lay side by side in the dirt.

The first intimation the engine crew had of Helen's arrival was the sound of her light step on the iron ladder entering the cab.

They turned—to look into the muzzle of a .30-.30 carbine.

"Get this train started!" ordered Helen Gorine, her voice cold and deadly. "Move—*fast!*"

With a startled grunt the Union Pacific hoghead released his brakes and pulled out the throttle bar.

Smoke erupted with a violent snort from the funnel-shaped stack. Drive wheels churned on the rails. Then the death train lunged forward into Bitterroot Cut, belching sparks and smoke.

Lieutenant Colonel Sires spun about from the gruesome task of making sure the last squad victim was dead, and yelled in dismay as he saw the train puff into the cut of the ridge, empty flatcar and red-painted jailcar gliding behind it.

The twelve troopers, white-faced from their

ordeal, could only stand in stupefied amazement as the train vanished around the curving rails.

Helen Gorine planted herself in the cab door, her rifle following the trembling fireman as he brought a load of cordwood from the jouncing tender.

"I'm not going to hurt anyone," she called out above the roar of the engine exhaust. "But get up speed, Mr. Hoghead! You'll stop when I tell you to!"

The engineer glanced over his shoulder and retorted:

"You'll catch hell for this lady. End-of-track is only eleven miles up the line, so you'd better think fast!"

Helen clung to a hand rail and peered up the track.

"See that lodgepole pine grove up ahead?" she shouted. "Stop alongside those trees."

The engineer reduced speed, finally grated to a steam-blowing halt alongside the grove of trees bordering the right of way.

"Now, get out!" ordered Helen Gorine as they turned to face her once more. "Start walking due south—and don't try anything funny while you're in rifle range. I can use this gun."

The jumper-clad trainmen made haste to obey the girl's command. Not until they were a hundred yards distant from the roadbed did Helen descend from the engine cab.

She jerked rifle to shoulder as she saw the startled jailcar guard walking up the track side to determine the cause of their unscheduled run toward end-of-track.

Sight of a lone girl, instead of the engine crew, completely unnerved the guard.

"Drop that pistol!" cried Helen Gorine. "Now, get back inside that car! Obey orders and you won't get hurt."

The trembling guard scrambled up into the jailcar, eyes wide with terror. Helen Gorine followed him, rifle poised defensively as the guard turned to face her with uplifted arms.

"Don't shoot, ma'am!" he begged piteously. "I got a fam—"

"Unlock Preston's cell!"

"But—ma'am—I'd be shot for treason if I let a pris—"

"Open that cell!"

The guard jumped to do her bidding. A moment later Quent Preston, a wide grin on his face, emerged from his iron-barred cage. Whipping the ring of keys from the guard's hand, he locked the quaking sentry inside the cell.

"That'll take care of him, Helen," drawled the Texan as the two jumped to the ground.

"Get started, Quent," she panted. "Your horse and mine are picketed in a draw over that hill yonder. Hurry!"

Quent Preston headed off across the rock-

146

strewn prairie, while Helen stooped to peer under the jail-car. She saw the engineer and fireman still running to the southward of the abandoned locomotive, well out of rifle range but still obeying orders.

Pausing only long enough to pick up the guard's army pistol, Helen set out after Quent Preston. She overtook him at the foot of the hillside, flushed and panting.

"The soldiers will be coming," she gasped. "Hurry—"

Preston grabbed her left hand and together they scaled the gentle slope until they were at the summit. A mile to the east they could see the firing squad riders galloping up the tracks toward the stalled train.

"Helen," panted the cowboy, "I never saw—the like—of this. How'd you manage—to get Alamo?"

She adjusted the chin strap of her Stetson, and, for the first time in twenty-four hours, the tense muscles of her face relaxed.

"I told the man—at the livery barn—I was your sister," she laughed. "Brought the horses—up here—last night. Spent the night—waiting at Bitterroot Cut—died a thousand deaths for fear— Colonel Sires would change the place and order of execution that I found out he planned."

Having recovered their wind, the two fugitives headed down the south slope. In a dry coulee a hundred yards below, Preston came upon his claybank pony, tethered in a patch of grass alongside Helen Gorine's leggy sorrel mustang.

"Just what," wheezed the cowboy as they dragged saddles aboard their mounts, "do we do next? I'm sort of mixed up like—"

She shrugged, busy putting a split-ear headstall over her mount's head.

"The only place—I can call home—is daddy's survey camp," she said. "But Quent—I've got to get back—to Wagonwheel City—when they bury dad—"

They swung into saddle, Helen booting her rifle and handing Preston the railway guard's .45-caliber revolver.

"Listen, Helen," said the Texan as they spurred off down the sloping ravine stirrup by stirrup, "we've got to think fast. I'll head for Tomahawk Pass and see you after things blow over. You—ride back to the railroad tracks. Colonel Sires won't court-martial a girl, the daughter of his old friend. Explain everything—he'll let you go back to town."

They reined up, man and girl locking glances for a long moment.

And in that fateful look Quent Preston realized with shocking suddenness that this sun-bronzed girl, so much a part of the wild frontier, was a part of him—something he could never give up, something vital to his future.

But there was no hint of his stabbing emotion in the handclasp he gave the girl.

"Hasta la vista, Helen," he smiled. "No use—tryin' to thank you for all this—when we're in such a hurry. I don't reckon I'll ever catch up thanking you, after today. *Adios!"*

She smiled, her eyes clinging to his.

"So long, Quent. I'd do it again—for you—any day."

He reined westward and spurred savagely so that she would not see his twitching face and guess what lay behind his torrent of emotions. When he had gained the west ridge of the ravine, he turned to wave at the girl who was climbing back toward the ridge crest on her way to the railroad.

His shout of farewell turned into a hoarse yell of horror.

For Preston's sun-squinted eyes recoiled before the heart-freezing vision of twenty-odd riders who appeared on the skyline, like teeth on a comb, in close-ranked formation on the eastern spur of the ravine.

"Indians!"

Morning sun rays gleamed off coppery, naked backs. To Quent's horrified ears came the awful whoop of Sioux death cries as the two dozen warriors, riding bareback on fleet Indian ponies, swept down the opposite side of the ravine toward Helen Gorine.

There was no time for her to gain the top of the hill. She caught sight of the Indians who bore down upon her at the same instant that Quent Preston spun his horse about and raced in her direction.

Frantically the girl tried to wave him back as she bent over her saddle and headed her sorrel toward the dry wash.

Smoke puffs came from Indian guns. Bullets kicked up dirt in front of Quent Preston's horse, peppered the ground on all sides of Helen Gorine's sorrel.

Then, with an oath of dismay, Quent Preston saw the girl's mustang falter, hard hit by Indian slugs.

Before it had traveled a dozen yards, Helen Gorine's mount toppled, mortally wounded.

Roweling Alamo to the peak of the Texas horse's limit of speed, Quent Preston sped down the hill as he saw Helen leap free of her falling horse.

An arrow zipped across the V-shaped trough of the ravine and imbedded itself in Alamo's withers, causing the claybank to squeal piteously and break its rhythmic stride.

Preston tore the flint-headed arrow out of his horse's flesh with his left hand, while the right cocked the .45 army pistol.

Then he was skidding Alamo to a dusty halt and leaning far out from saddle to encircle Helen Gorine in the powerful crook of his left arm.

"My horse—fell on top of rifle—couldn't save it," she gasped, swinging astride Alamo's saddle cantle behind Preston. "But Quent—you shouldn't have come back—impossible for us to both make it—carrying double—"

In a flurry of dust and screaming bullets, Preston wheeled Alamo and headed for the west slope. But already the whooping Indian band had divided, ten yowling riders plunging across the pit of the ravine and riding out on the western slope to cut off their escape.

Preston reined downhill, but saw a flying line of naked Sioux warriors closing up that route. Behind him were more Indians, their bows twanging as they sent arrows swarming down in a lethal hail upon the encircled couple.

"We're surrounded, Helen," gasped Preston. "No chance for both of us—you get in saddle—try to make top of hill—"

Preston's cry was cut short as a Sioux arrow knocked him from saddle and landed him, face down, on the ground, the arrow quivering from his back muscles like a plucked fiddle string.

Helen Gorine flung herself from the horse, dragging the pony's reins as she headed back toward the fallen cowboy. Even as she did so the war-bonneted chief of the Indian band flashed by, hurling a feather-hung tomahawk straight at the girl's skull.

It was Alamo, Preston's claybank cow pony that

151

saved Helen Gorine's life in the clock-tick of time which followed.

The pony, rearing back to avoid collision with the war chief's oncoming mount, jerked so violently on the reins which the girl had looped about her left wrist that it halted her rush and knocked her off her feet.

The hard-flung tomahawk sped past the spot which an instant before had been occupied by Helen's skull and caromed off a rock with a splintering of its wooden handle.

Staggering to her knees, Helen Gorine crawled to Preston's side as the wounded Texan propped himself off the ground with one elbow and fumbled groggily at the embedded arrow in his back.

"Quent—don't—oh, Quent—"

Luckily, the sharp flint arrowhead had entered his body at an angle and had deflected along a rib, otherwise it would have embedded itself, heart-deep, through the cowboy's lung.

Wincing, Preston snapped off the arrow's shaft several inches above the blood-spurting wound under his buckskin shirt. He well knew the uselessness of trying to wrench the barbed obsidian point out of his flesh. That would require a knife.

Throwing the feather-tipped shaft of the arrow aside, Preston groped in the dust for the Colt .45 which had been jarred from his grasp when he was knocked from horseback.

Cocking the hammer with a thumb, the Texan drew aim at the paint-bedaubed Sioux chief when the savage, realizing that his tomahawk had missed its target, skidded his pony to a halt and raced back toward the spot where the white man and woman crouched in the swirling dust.

The chief's eagle-feathered war bonnet bannered in the wind behind him as he charged up, shifting a rifle from his left hand to his right for a close-range shot.

Lining his revolver sights on the Indian's hideous visage, Preston squeezed trigger. Through belching gun smoke he saw the Sioux lurch backward on his horse, head drilled by a slug.

Then the slain chief toppled over the rump of his galloping mount, landing with a heavy impact not fifty feet from where Preston knelt.

Again Preston fired, this time sending his high calibered slug into the brisket of the Sioux's horse before it could run him and Helen down with flailing hoofs.

The pony collapsed, rolling over with threshing legs pointed skyward, then sagged over on its side a scant six feet away.

The other Indians were galloping in a tightening circle about the ravine, closing in swiftly on their doomed quarry.

Seizing Helen's arm, Quent Preston crawled rapidly forward and bore her down behind the scant shelter of the dead animal. Billowing dust was their only protection now.

Through the sifting screen of alkali particles, the two could see the screeching warriors riding in closer, holding their fire as they tightened their ring of doom.

"It'll be a short fight," muttered Preston. "But we'll take a few Injuns with us—"

Resting his pistol barrel across the Indian pony's carcass, Preston triggered the .45 a third time, saw a yowling Sioux brave hurl up his arms and topple off his bareback pony, to lay kicking amid a boulder nest, a bullet lodged in his groin.

Quent Preston swabbed perspiration out of his eyes with a buckskin sleeve and raised his head above the level of the dead horse's barrel for a glance around. Their lot was clearly hopeless, surrounded and outnumbered as they were.

A dozen savages were approaching from the rear, veering toward the chief's corpse.

Fifty feet away, in the open, was the dead chief's carbine; but Preston knew it would be impossible to get the rifle without being cut down by a hail of slugs.

He jacked open the Colt in his hands. Only two bullets remained in the chambers; the other cartridges were empty.

Two slugs—enough, he reasoned grimly, to put Helen and himself beyond the threat of a Sioux torture stake.

Trying to close his brain against the horror of what he must do, Preston snapped the cylinder back into its frame, spun it into place.

He turned to Helen Gorine, who was still clinging to Alamo's bridle reins. A fearsome look was in the cowboy's glance as he met the girl's eyes.

Horror was mirrored there, but this stanch daughter of the frontier was showing courage under fire as they faced inevitable doom.

"Helen," choked the Texan, "you know—how Sioux treat white women they take prisoner?"

She nodded, eyes clogged with tears.

"Then—forgive me—and God forgive me—for doing this!"

Before the girl could divine the meaning of his choked words, Quent Preston pressed the gun muzzle against Helen's heart, shut his eyes against the horror to come, and pulled trigger—

XXII

SCALPING KNIFE

THE hollow click of a firing pin striking a shell which had already been fired met Preston's ears. A shock of nausea went through the Texan, as he realized that in twirling the gun's cylinder when he thrust it back into its frame, he had accidentally put a used shell under the hammer.

Before he could cock the single-action weapon again, he was struck heavily by a naked warrior who had dived off his horse in passing. Copper-skinned arms locked in a strangle hold about his neck. Two more warriors pounced off their horses to seize Helen Gorine before she could get the Colt out of Preston's hand.

A rifle butt lifted and fell, striking Preston's head with a grisly thud. He went limp. The paint-smeared Indian who had jumped upon him relaxed his strangling grip and gave vent to a soul-curdling yell of triumph.

Dizzily, Preston looked about him. His blurred gaze found Helen just as he was hoisted to his feet by powerful arms. Then he was dragged bodily to the spot where fifteen or more of the Indians had gathered about the body of their slain chief.

The air was a din of sound as a sub-chief

confirmed the fact of their leader's death. Then, simultaneously, the mourning cries of the Sioux gave way to a ghastly hush.

A battery of eyes swung to cover the white captives under a withering glare.

Helen and Preston were dragged forward. The cowboy knew the meaning of this ominous silence. Their doom had been irrevocably sealed when he had shot the war-bonneted chief of the band.

Helen would undoubtedly be taken captive to a Sioux camp, there to meet an unthinkable fate, with eventual torture and death. Preston would be butchered on the spot, scalped, and his corpse left on this desolate hillside to be mutilated by coyotes.

A Sioux with white and yellow ochre smeared on his hawklike nose and protruding cheekbones was hunkered over the dead chief, chanting a husky Indian death ritual. From the three feathers stuck in his black topknot, Preston knew this was a secondary chieftain, but now in full command of the war party.

The assembled warriors growled with the guttural accents of wild beasts as the kneeling Indian gently removed the eagle-feathered bonnet from the chief's head, and placed it on his own in token of his new authority.

Then, with eyes flashing like twin pools of fire, the new chief stood up. One coppery fist closed over the hilt of a bowie knife in his rawhide-thonged belt. The belt was festooned with grisly hanks of vari-colored hair. Human scalps! The scalps of white victims.

Helen Gorine cried out in horror as she saw the Sioux turn slowly to impale Quent Preston with his glare.

As the Sioux chief put one moccasin-clad foot forward, Preston's two captors dropped his limp body to the ground. In falling the Texan's eyes met Helen's, his vision still dimmed by the stunning blow he had received a moment before.

With an inhuman screech, the Sioux pounced like a cougar upon the fallen white. The splayed fingers of his left hand clamped into the Texan's hair, and Preston's head was lifted off the ground.

Helen went faint as she saw that Quent was to die the most horrible death a white man could know here on the plains: that of being scalped alive. Preston's eyes and tongue would follow, trophies of the infuriated Sioux's butcher knife.

Preston was powerless to move a muscle, paralyzed by the fatal blaze in the Indian's slitted eyes.

The scalper's foul breath was hot on his face. The Indian's teeth ground together in the passion of his rage, as he thrust his scalping knife against the flesh of Preston's brow, a quarter inch below the hairline.

The razor-honed knife sliced through the skin

of his forehead and hit bone with the scalding agony of a naked flame.

And then the Sioux snatched back his knife and dropped his grip on Preston's hair, as a frantic yell of warning came from one of the circling warriors.

Helen Gorine stared past the heads about her and saw the reason for the scalper's sudden halt.

Pounding over the top of the hill above them came twelve uniformed members of the army firing squad, riding in pursuit—as they thought— of Helen Gorine and their escaped prisoner, Quent Preston.

The U. S. cavalrymen halted in dismay as they saw the Indians on the slope below them. Then Colonel Sires shouted a harsh command, and the mounted troops opened fire on the Indians grouped on the hillside.

Quent Preston's veins were charged with sudden vitality, as new hope flashed through his mind.

He drew back his legs and kicked violently upward, his high-heeled cowboots catching the Indian chief in the stomach even as the Sioux chief leaned down to hack off another scalp trophy before joining his braves in flight.

With a grunt of pain, the Sioux staggered backward, the scalping knife flashing in the sun. A curtain of blood threaded down over Preston's eyes from the cut in his scalp, so that he did not get the satisfaction of seeing a cavalryman's bullet chug into the Indian's heart and drop him in his tracks.

Helen Gorine's captors had released the girl and were running for their horses.

With high-pitched yells of baffled rage, the score of surviving Indians headed down the ravine on their ponies. Preston saw three more Indians pitch from their horses' backs before the last of the Sioux melted into a coulee and were gone.

Preston was helped to his feet by Helen Gorine. He swabbed blood out of his eyelashes and grinned as the two clung to each other, shutting their eyes against the ghastly shambles about them.

"Helen, you weren't born to cash in your chips today," panted the cowboy finally, as they looked up the hill where the victorious troops were riding down to meet them. "You . . . you understood why I was going to . . . to shoot—"

"Yes, Quent," whispered the girl, her head close against his shoulder. "Both of us brushed mighty close, then—"

Colonel Sires and his firing-squad riders reined up beside them. The hard-faced old army man stared about at the grim evidence of the melee—red-skinned corpses sprawled grotesquely amid the rocks and sagebrush, arrows and guns and a broken hatchet littering the foot-trampled scene.

"We've no time to wait here!" cried the army commander. "Those Indians had us outnumbered two to one as it was—they thought we were just the forerunners of a big detachment, or they would have stood us off."

Preston caught Alamo and helped Helen into the saddle, then mounted behind the cantle.

Colonel Sires, wise in the way of Indian war tactics, knew that Helen and Preston had run afoul of a mere scouting party. Undoubtedly there was a big concentration of warriors out in the hills not far away.

"We've got to hurry back and board the train," ordered Sires, as they headed back toward the hill crest. "I haven't the slightest doubt but that those Injuns will bring back the rest of their war party, on the double."

Preston noticed that the cavalrymen ringed their horses about his in a tight convoy as they left the bloody scene. He knew that both he and Helen, though they were being rescued by these men, were, nevertheless, military prisoners.

XXIII

FLIGHT ON THE IRON HORSE

THE cavalcade finally reached the train just as the sheepish engineer and fireman returned to duty in their cab.

"We'll have to leave our horses here!" said Colonel Sires briskly, as they dismounted in the shadow of the engine. "We're sure to be attacked by Indians before we can get back to Wagonwheel City, if I'm any judge of Sioux tricks. We haven't time to load our mounts on the railway car here."

Preston downed a hard lump in his throat as he dismounted from Alamo for the last time. He had raised the claybank from a colt, trained it as if it were a human partner. Now it would be turned loose on the open range, possibly to become the property of some cruel Indian.

"Adios, Alamo pard!" whispered the cowboy, lifting his saddle skirt to untie the latigo.

Then, before he could slip bridle and saddle from the pony, Colonel Sires was ordering him inside the jailcar.

The soldiers, with anxious glances up at the northern ridge behind him, clambered into the car after Helen and Preston were aboard. Then the sliding door was shut, the engineer threw his

162

reverse lever and whistled twice, and the train headed back toward the east.

Preston shuddered as he saw the open cell doors. No prisoners cowered there now. He sat down on one of the sentry's chairs, while Helen Gorine bent over him and set to work to extract the Sioux arrowhead from the flesh of his back.

"A narrow escape, that one," commented Colonel Sires, swaying on outspread feet to the jouncing of the car. "I've seen a Sioux arrow completely impale a man."

Preston grinned wryly.

"You saved my hair, colonel," he gritted through the pain, "but the way things stack up, you saved me from the frying pan to . . . to put me in the fire."

Sires coughed, swallowing hard.

"Duty is duty," he said. "I'm not going to push any charge against Miss Gorine, here. Her prank of kidnapping this train was wild and absurd, but she did it out of a woman's love for you, no doubt. We will consider her punished enough by the fact that her foolish escapade to save you from the firing squad has . . . er . . . ended in a failure."

Helen shuddered as she finished worming the Sioux arrowhead out of Preston's lacerated flesh. But it had been the colonel's oblique way of repeating Quent's death sentence that occasioned the involuntary shudder.

"The execution will be postponed until tomorrow," went on the colonel. "We have to get back to Wagonwheel City—to clear the tracks for the workers and the troop train headed for railhead, as well as to escape another Sioux attack."

Preston nodded his thanks for the brief reprieve. He was likewise grateful for the fact that Sires had not handcuffed him again. At least, during the brief five-mile ride back to the construction camp, he would be with Helen. The warmth of her presence made him forget the pain of his wounds.

The train made a brief halt at Bitterroot Cut, to pick up the soldier whose horse Colonel Sires had appropriated for the chase, and the other jailcar guard.

Both men tossed shovels into the car ahead of them. As the train got under way once more, Preston counted three shallow mounds over by the cutbank.

Seiden, Bates, Leacock—three more graves in the long, long chain of mounds along the Union Pacific line to Omaha. He wondered if his own grave would be here at Bitterroot Cut within another twenty-four hours.

His grisly thought was interrupted by a piercing shriek of the locomotive whistle, and a lurch of the jail car as the engineer opened his throttle wider.

Soldiers rushed to the barred windows of the, jail car, and Quent Preston saw the cause for their blanched faces and chorus of oaths as he and Helen looked out on the Wyoming landscape.

A tremendous Sioux war party, numbering over two hundred, swept out of a brush-flanked canyon bordering the tracks and closed in toward the train, guns flashing, lungs whooping.

Every rider was plastered against the outside of his pony's body in the trick of horsemanship mastered by the plains Indians, offering only one foot and an arm to shoot at.

Above the snorting of the locomotive and the rattle of cars over the unleveled tracks came the thunderous concussion of rifle fire, and bullets peppered the wooden walls of the car.

"We're in for it!" shouted Colonel Sires. "They've probably set fire to that three-mile trestle. Choose windows and return their fire, men—shoot their horses!"

The uniformed soldiers leaped to the tiny barred windows, thrust rifles outside, and began shooting.

Preston's hands itched for a gun as he saw that the soldiers were seemingly unable to hit the flying targets alongside the laboring train.

Gradually the Sioux dropped back as the train outraced the fleet ponies on the uneven ground. The savages began concentrating their attack on the engineer's cab.

Quent seized Helen's arm and raced with her to the forward end of the lurching jailcar. There were two windows there overlooking the flatcar outside and the long V of the unblasted railroad tracks, curving in graceful S's through the hills. Soon the construction town at Wagonwheel Springs would swing in view, two miles in the distance.

"We're safe!" cried Preston in relief, his lips against Helen's ear. "Unless that trestle's been fired—"

"For once," laughed Helen Gorine, "you must be glad you're riding an Iron Horse, Quent. It's the only thing I know of that could outrun an Injun pony!"

But Preston, unlike Colonel Sires, had not figured on the ruthless cunning of the red men. Even as he stared out at the curving tracks ahead, he caught sight of four feathered Sioux grouped on a sharp curve dead ahead.

The Indians were heaping a barricade of cull railroad crossties across the rails. As they saw the train thundering down upon them from westward, they leaped off the roadbed and vanished into screening chaparral.

Preston spun to yell a warning at the soldiers in the car:

"Look out—we're going off the tracks—"

The cowboy grabbed Helen and swung her in front of him so that her body would be shielded by his when the crash came. Glancing out the end window, the wind whipping his eyes, Preston saw the end of the flatcar hit the pile of ties.

There was a thunderous crash as the flatcar bounded skyward. One set of wheel trucks bounded off to the north while the flatcar careened and gouged a corner into the cutbank.

The jailcar reared aloft like a ship in a heavy tempest. Too late, the engineer had jammed on his puny brakes.

For an instant there was chaos as the jailcar capsized and struck the smooth dirt of the sloping bank. Preston got a kaleidoscopic glimpse of soldiers being flung like straw dummies about the overturning car.

His ears registered the appalling crash of wood, the din of metal on rock, exploding steam, men screaming, all rising in a curdling crescendo of catastrophe.

Then all was blotted out as momentum crushed Helen Gorine against his chest.

Hot sunlight was in Preston's eyes as he shook himself dazedly back to his senses.

He was lying on the splintered remains of what had been the varnished ceiling panels of the jailcar.

Blue sky was a canopy above him. He was staring upward at a great hole which a boulder had torn out of the floor of the car. That meant the jailcar was resting upside down on its roof—

"Helen! Helen, are you—"

Then Preston caught sight of the girl, her body crisscrossing his numb legs. She was unconscious, but a strong pulse throbbed along her neck and Preston sobbed with relief as a quick inspection revealed no visible injury.

The pain in his own chest, where ribs had been cracked by the pressure, gave the Texan the reassurance that Helen's life had probably been saved by the fact that the impact of the train smash-up had been cushioned on his own body, instead of against the unyielding wood and iron of the car's end.

The triumphant whoops of Sioux warriors roused Preston to more immediate peril than their hurts.

He got to his feet, and stared along the broken interior of the jailcar. Shafts of sunlight poured through cracks and gaping holes in roof and walls, revealing a ghastly carnage.

Soldiers were sprawled here and there through the wreckage. The one nearest Preston had died of a broken neck. Another was horribly mangled where a fanglike boulder had smashed through the roof of the car to crush him.

Colonel Sires lay groaning with a broken arm a few feet away. Dust and smoke filled the car with a smudge which hid from Preston's view the dead or dying farther back.

The twisted door of a cell made a natural ladder

up to the hole in the floor plankings, and Preston climbed up the steel latticework to stick his head outside.

The locomotive lay on its side, its boiler as crinkled as a stovepipe elbow. A geyser of steam erupted through an unriveted seam; the scalded corpse of the engineer hung jackknifed over the matchwood that had been the windowsill of his cab.

Coals from the broken grates had been scattered here and there and had ignited Russian thistle and sagebrush along the right-of-way. Flames were crackling ominously and lifting a thin haze of smoke to blend with the dense white clouds of steam.

Then Preston stiffened as he saw four Sioux warriors skulking along the drivewheels of the demolished engine, knives in hand, hunting in the tangled debris for victims to scalp. They were working toward the shattered jail car where the bulk of their prey would be found.

Preston ducked back inside the wrecked car and crawled through splintered timbers and twisted iron until he came to a dead soldier, grasping a rifle.

Unprying the gun from taut fingers, Preston turned back toward the gaping hole overhead.

Then he gasped as the feathered shadow of an Indian fell like a blot of doom upon Helen Gorine's insensible form.

XXIV

PARTNERS OF THE WILDS

IRING almost straight up, Quent Preston drove a bullet through the warrior's skull even as the Sioux braced himself to jump down into the car.

With a gagged cry, the Indian toppled down through the gaping hole in the car's floor and landed with a sodden thud at Preston's feet.

The concussion of the rifle shot inside the car brought a series of wild yells from the other three savages who were exploring the wrecked train.

Levering another shell into the army gun, Preston climbed up the slanting cell door once more and peered outside.

Spang! He ducked as a bullet made a long, smoking furrow through the wood—inches from his head.

Then the cowboy shoved his rifle barrel over the selfsame bullet groove and caught sight of a Sioux buck desperately reloading his one-shot rifle, behind the still-spinning wheels at the back of the car.

Preston fired, saw the Indian sag back with a bullet-smashed shoulder. Before the warrior could crawl out of sight Preston finished the job with another slug.

Then the cowboy's veins congealed with dread as wind whipped aside the pall of smoke and steam, to reveal the main Sioux war party galloping up from the west toward the wreckage.

Preston knew it would be hopeless for a lone man to stand off the onslaught of that mighty band of Sioux. It was doubtful if he would get any assistance from soldiers in the car; they had not had enough warning before the crash to brace themselves.

Bracing his rifle across a twisted brake rod, Preston drew long and careful bead on the foremost of the oncoming Indian horde, a painted chief with a billowing spread of feathers tailing out from behind his war bonnet.

When the Texan calculated the Indian was inside the range of the carbine, he squeezed trigger.

An exultant cry blew from his lips as he saw the Sioux's horse lurch and go down, throwing its rider. Preston's bullet, intended for the chief's breast, had gone low and drilled the galloping pony in the skull.

But the chief was killed instantly as he was catapulted on his head against the U. P. rail. His corpse and the floundering carcass of his horse were trampled under the oncoming tidal wave of mounted Indians.

The war party split, avoiding the open V of the tracks when they were within a hundred yards of the wrecked train. As yet they could not see the lone sharpshooter whose head was protruding above the floor of the upside-down jailcar.

The dense mass of drifting steam from the ruptured engine boiler might be hiding any number of defenders, for all the Indians knew.

Preston twisted his neck to eastward, and a low oath of thanksgiving burst from him as he saw a train pounding at full speed up the rails from Wagonwheel City!

"The troop train!" gasped the cowboy, his eyes slitted against the smoke from burning brush that was enveloping everything. "They'll scatter those damned Injuns double quick—"

A war whoop down inside the jailcar behind him made Preston drop hastily inside, his boots cushioned against the inert corpse of the brave he had shot.

A naked savage had crawled through the splintered door of the car and had seized Colonel Sires by the hair. The army man was just returning to consciousness, but offered no resistance as the Indian poised a scalping knife over his face.

Whipping rifle stock to cheek, Preston sent a bullet into the Indian's head at close range. The mushrooming slug nearly tore the Sioux's head from his body.

Preston's blood-smeared face relaxed in an ironic grin, as he saw the Indian collapse on top

172

of the colonel. Preston had saved the life of the very man who would be giving the order to execute him on the morrow!

The strident whistle of the approaching army train from Wagonwheel City blended with the yells of the encircling Indians.

Thudding hoofs rattled on the ground outside; the crackling of the flames through the brush added a sullen undertone to the babble of confusion.

Again Preston clambered up the cell-door ladder and looked outside. The troop train was slowing to a stop nearby; puffs of smoke and the crackle of gunnery came from the flatcars behind the locomotive, as blue-uniformed troops opened a deadly fusillade on the dismayed Indians.

The Sioux, however, had no intention of bucking an entire detachment of soldiery. They were already scattering into the hills, out of range.

The entire south slope of the right-of-way was ablaze now, from the brush which had been set afire by the coals flung out of the ruined firebox of the wrecked locomotive.

Smoke was beating over the wreck; Preston could not see fifty yards in any direction.

The troop train grated to a halt and hundreds of soldiers swarmed off the flatcars, dropping to their knees and blasting a terrific salvo toward the fleeing Sioux.

A moment later the entire band of Indians had vanished into the countless gullies and valleys, without appreciable losses.

Behind the troop train came the U. P. work train, laden with hundreds of iron-muscled Irish paddies headed for end-of-track. In a few moments, they would be adding to the crowds of men who would be picking through the wreckage of the jailcar.

They would find Preston among the others, would know from his cowboy costume that he was one of the four men slated to die before the firing squad at Bitterroot Cut. He would be promptly taken into custody again—

"No, damn it! I can vamose—"

Now that he had a moment's respite in which to think, Preston saw his chance at escape.

He took a quick glance about the jailcar. Colonel Sires was getting to his feet, his body drenched by the blood of the Indian who had so nearly scalped him as he lay helpless.

Sires would never know who had saved his life. Even if he was told that Preston had done just that, it would have been difficult for the stern old army man to believe.

The Texan's gaze flitted back to Helen Gorine. The girl still lay in the swath of smoke-dimmed sunlight, her flowing chestnut hair spread out over the shattered wooden panels.

Her eyelids were still shut, but a healthy glow

of color was returning to her relaxed features, indicating that she would be conscious again before very long.

"*Hasta la vista,* Helen!" whispered Quent Preston, gripping one of her limp hands in his own. "I got to be movin' now, but I'll see you again—someday—"

On a sudden impulse he stooped to kiss the girl lightly on the lips. Then he climbed up out onto the floor of the overturned jailcar, a floor which was now a roof.

The soldiers from the troop train were climbing the wreckage on three sides, now. But not one of them caught a glimpse of Preston's flitting figure as the cowboy jumped down off the car and darted into the heart of the flaming chaparral along the south side of the tracks.

He gulped lungfuls of clean air as he burrowed his way out of the blazing weeds and scrambled up the hill. There, under a sheltering outcrop of granite a good fifty feet above the roadbed, Preston lay on his stomach and peered down on the scene, safe from discovery.

Hundreds of Irishmen from the track gang were swarming amid the soldiers now. Shovels made short work of putting out the brush fire which threatened the wreckage. Then army officers were taking charge, their orders cracking like whips.

Colonel Sires was the first to be assisted out of

the wreckage. The grizzled old war dog was still too dazed to explain the circumstances of the Indian attack.

Excited yells came from the rescue squads as Helen Gorine, conscious now, was lifted tenderly out of the debris and carried toward the troop train.

Before she was out of the range of Preston's sight, he saw her set to her feet. She was wobbly-kneed, but able to walk.

For twenty minutes, confusion reigned on the roadbed below Preston's hide-out. Brawny Irish paddies bent their shoulders to the task of carrying obstacles off the track. Luckily, the bulky engine had hurtled itself completely clear of the rails.

Inside of half an hour the track was cleared and the troops began heading back for their train. A bell clanged; the troop-train engine gave two short blasts of its whistle; and the cars began rolling westward again. Train wrecks or Sioux attacks could not hinder the inexorable march of the U. P. toward the Pacific!

As Quent Preston lay in his ambush and watched the soldier-packed train move on by, the germ of an idea soared into his brain. Following the troop train would be the work train, laden with throngs of redshirted and blue-shirted Irish paddies. On the rear of that train were a dozen flat cars loaded with rails and ties and machinery.

Preston crawled on hands and knees down the smoking hillside until he was once more to the jailcar. He made his way through the littered wreckage until he came to the overturned engine.

There he crouched, watching as the locomotive of the work train snorted past, not six feet from where he was hidden.

One by one he counted the flatcars, loaded to capacity with singing Irishmen.

Finally the flats gave way to cars stacked high with fresh ties for end-of-track, and back of them three cars loaded with steel rails and scores of kegs filled with spikes, fishplates and other equipment necessary for bridging a continent with steel.

When the front wheels of the tail-end car rolled past him, Preston stepped into the open, his body hidden from possible eyes by the clouds of steam which still billowed from the smashed engine.

Running along the roadbed, Preston grabbed hold of a hand bar and swung himself catlike aboard the footrail at the end of the train.

He clung there, wind whipping his hair and cooling his face, out of sight of the workmen on the cars up front.

Miles ticked by, as the work train added its smoke to the black feather of smudge left by the troop train ahead. Bitterroot Cut swung out behind, its three grave mounds casting shadows on the sand.

Not until he saw the clump of lodgepole pines where Helen Gorine had halted the jail train did Preston prepare to leave the train on which he had stolen a ride.

Picking out a soft pile of dirt shoveled away to level the roadbed, the cowboy jumped. He landed rolling to come up short against a cushioning bed of sage.

He lay panting a few minutes, until the train had vanished in the distance. Then he got shakily to his feet, swatting dust from his bat-wing chaps and buckskin shirt.

The leap off the train had not injured him. Now his only concern was to locate a horse among the thirteen mustangs which Colonel Sires had abandoned at this place. But that would not be difficult. Even as he walked out toward the pine grove, he saw Alamo grazing in a patch of bluestem there.

"Alamo, old pardner! Come along here, boy!"

The horse pranced with excitement as it recognized its master. Grazing here and there about the plain were the army horses, still bridled and saddled. Of Indians Preston saw no trace; he doubted if they dared show up again in the vicinity during that day, at least.

Ten minutes later, Preston was aboard his Texas pony once more and headed northwestward toward Tomahawk Pass.

A consummate sense of victory overcame the

throb of his broken ribs and the arrow wound in his back. For he was free—reunited with his four-footed partner of the wilds. No enemy could overtake him now, be it a Wagonwheel soldier or a Sioux!

With a gay Texas range melody on his lips, his heart welling with joy and a will to live for the first time in the bitter weeks since the U. P. R. had come to rob him of peace and elbow room, Quent Preston headed out on a long lope across the hills toward his Lone Star Ranch in the rugged Sioux Bonnets.

XXV

HOMESTEAD PAPERS

THAT afternoon a U. P. locomotive returned to Wagonwheel City bringing with it Colonel Sires and Helen Gorine. And inside the hour a full account of the Indian attack on the jail train was rolling off the press of the Wagonwheel City *Gazette,* a weekly paper published by a tramp printer who followed the westering rails with his hand press and other equipment. The sheet had been variously known, back along the U. P. R., as the *Gazette* of Laramie, Cheyenne, North Platte, and Kearney.

The newspaper story was greeted by the construction town in various ways ranging from rank indifference to feverish excitement. And it caused Boone Delivan to look up a pair of buffalo-coated gunhawks and make his way down the main street with grim purpose behind his swift strides.

Delivan swung off the street and entered Ellis Bayard's Land Office without knocking. The front room was deserted; a gunnysack rug had been tacked on the floor to hide the black stains of Lige Morton's blood.

Delivan jerked open the partition door, to find Ellis Bayard on his knees before a half-packed carpetbag. The speculator's lips curled in a sneer of contempt as he barked out:

"I thought so, Bayard. Leaving town, eh?"

The bald-headed attorney looked up with his pendant jowls trembling under brown muttonchop whiskers. His gaze widened with concern as he saw the two rock-eyed bodyguards behind Delivan.

"You're damned right I'm getting out, Boone. You should be heading out of Wagonwheel City yourself. Haven't you read this afternoon's copy of the *Gazette*?"

Boone Delivan jabbed a hand into his frock coat and drew out a rumpled copy of the paper.

"Hell, yes. Interesting wasn't it? All about Colonel Sires breaking an arm when the Sioux ditched his jail train. I also see an item about the mysterious knifing of Major John Gorine. But why should you get in a lather and start packing?"

Bayard heaved his corpulent bulk erect with a grunt of effort, and snatched the paper from Delivan's hands. The lawyer pointed an ague-stricken finger to a news item on the front page and read a paragraph therefrom in a tremulous voice:

"—one of the peculiar sidelights to this mornin's train wreck is the fact that the escaped prisoner, Quentin Preston, was nowhere to be found in the wreckage. Officers

181

say it is doubtful that the Sioux took him captive, as the prompt arrival of the U. P. troop train prevented any looting or scalping."

Raw fear was in Bayard's eyes as he shoved the *Gazette* back into the speculator's hand.

"You see what that means, don't you?" moaned the lawyer, his moonlike face sticky with sweat. *"It means Preston escaped."*

"Preston escaped!" echoed Delivan nastily. "Thanks to Helen Gorine! O. K.—why should Preston's getaway agitate *you?*"

Bayard caught the menace in Delivan's tone, and his voice changed to a whine:

"Boone—the first thing that Texas hellion will do will be to come back to Wagonwheel City— and go gunning for you and me! H-he knows we framed Morton's killing onto him and he'll chase us to the brink of hell to get revenge!"

Evil lights flickered in Delivan's eyes. He turned to Jeb Franklin, a coarse-featured owl-hooter from the Mexican-border country who had come to the U. P. to rent his six-guns.

"There's a train leaving Wagonwheel City for Omaha today, Franklin. Make sure Bayard isn't aboard it."

The lawyer groaned with panic.

"What . . . what do you intend to do, Boone?"

Delivan jerked a thumb toward his other bodyguard.

"Jim Randle and I are riding out to Tomahawk Pass after those homestead papers of Preston's. We'll dig them up first thing in the morning, before Preston beats us to it. And you, my dear Bayard, are the shyster who is going to forge those deeds over to me, understand?"

Bayard tried to swallow his terror. He smirked in a ghastly way and rubbed his moist palms greedily.

"Of course, of course. I hadn't forgotten our . . . deal. The U. P. will pay us fifty thousand for the right-of-way through Tomahawk Pass, rather than fight us in the courts and tie up their construction gangs before they get a condemnation order. We'll make a fortune, Boone."

Delivan turned on his heel and brushed past Franklin, who sat down on Bayard's cot and calmly helped himself to a bottle of the lawyer's bourbon.

Leaving the land office, Delivan and his gun-hung henchman went to the Overland Livery Barn, where hostlers saddled mustangs for them.

Leaving Wagonwheel City behind, the two riders followed the Union Pacific rails until midafternoon. Then they veered off to the north, taking the trail which Delivan had often traveled on his visits to Major John Gorine's survey camp.

Indian sign was numerous, and the white puffs of Sioux signal fires on hill crags to the northward made them leave the traveled trail and keep out of sight in the valleys. Night overtook them twenty miles from Gorine's camp.

"What if we cross trails with that Preston hombre, boss?" inquired Jim Randle, as they were saddling up next morning at dawn.

Delivan's nostrils flared. He was thinking of Helen Gorine at the moment, and his thoughts were not pleasant ones.

"I'll take care of Preston. No man ever dared steal a girl from Boone Delivan, but Preston stole mine—without knowing he did. That's why I'll put a bullet in Preston's guts—myself."

The sun was three hours high by the time Delivan and Randle halted at the tents belonging to Major Gorine's survey camp. They found Henderson and Fischer, two of the engineers, busy drafting.

"Howdy, Delivan!" greeted Henderson. "We just heard about Gorine's murder. It was hell—the major just at the climax of his greatest triumph. Know any of the details?"

Delivan shook his head, then inquired anxiously:

"How'd you hear about Gorine's death so soon?"

"Quent Preston spent the night in our camp. The cowboy was pretty well spent—had a brush with the Injuns yesterday."

Delivan and Randle exchanged sharp glances.

"Where's Preston now?"

Henderson pointed up the trail.

"Left for his ranch an hour ago."

Without further talk, Delivan spurred on through the camp and headed off past Linn DePerren's grave at trailside, going at a gallop. Jim Randle was following at his heels. Soon they were emerging out onto the level rangeland of the Lone Star Ranch. Only then did Boone Delivan realize the overwhelming damage which his raiders, under Bob Averill, had done to Preston's spread.

The ruffian at his stirrup, Jim Randle, was one of the three men who had returned from that raid alive. It had been Randle's .30-.30 that had downed Weldon, the traitor whose testimony against Delivan had so nearly ended the latter's career.

"Did a thorough job—outside of nailing Preston for me," grunted the speculator, shielding his eyes against the sun and scanning the fire-blackened range. "Come on."

Delivan's mouth twitched with pent-up rage as they headed toward the ash heaps which had been Preston's homestead buildings. If a man wanted a thing done right, Delivan was thinking, he must do it himself. That was why he was attending to the job of filching Preston's homestead papers personally.

Between them and the site of Preston's ranchhouse was a thick copse of box elder trees,

185

now black skeletons as a result of the fire which had ravaged Tomahawk Pass.

As the two crooks emerged from the trees, they caught sight of a lone man digging amid the ruins of the log cabin, his back to them. Hitched to the gaunt fireplace chimney was a familiar claybank pony.

"That's Preston!" snarled Delivan, snaking a Winchester saddle gun from its scabbard under his right knee. "A hundred bucks to you, Randle, if you tally him!"

Even as they halted their horses and lifted rifles to shoulders, Quent Preston paused in his work and looked around.

Crrrrash! The rifles thundered in the silence of the devastated valley. Bullets kicked up spurts of dry ashes about Quent Preston's boots, as he stood stockstill amid the ruins of his home.

Preston took one look at the two horsemen firing at him from a hundred-yard range, and knew he was trapped in the open with no available shelter closer than the north river bank.

With a low cry of anger, the Texan headed for his horse, bullets humming about him as the two killers pumped their rifle levers and fired savage bursts in his direction.

Vaulting into Alamo's saddle, Quent Preston headed down the slope to the river, sped down its shallow bank and splashed across.

"He hasn't a rifle, or he'd have gotten behind

the chimney and used it!" yelled Boone Delivan, spurring his mount into a gallop. "You keep him at bay, Randle—I know what Preston was doing in those ashes!"

Quent Preston gained the north bank of Beavertail River, with Jim Randle peppering his back trail with .30-.30 slugs. He was ducking into thick willow growth just as Delivan leaped off his horse beside the ruined cabin.

A yell of triumph came from the speculator's lips as he saw that Quent Preston had been in the act of prying up a flat granite slab from the fireplace hearth.

"He told Bayard he'd cached his valuable papers under the house—damned if that isn't where—"

Running forward, Delivan pried down the fire-blackened crowbar which Preston had dropped at the moment of his attack.

The flat chunk of granite pried upward under the leverage, to reveal a hollowed-out place under the hearth.

An oblong tin box, undamaged by the conflagration which had razed the cabin, lay in the exposed cavity. Even as he snatched up the box and broke it open against the sooty mantel, Boone Delivan knew his victory was won.

Inside a thick paper envelope was a document heavy with seals and bearing the signature of Abraham Lincoln, President of the United States of America. That paper was the sole proof which Quent Preston possessed to the ownership of his homestead here in Tomahawk Pass.

Stuffing the precious deed in his frock-coat pocket, Boone Delivan raced back to his horse and mounted.

Across the river, Quent Preston was still hidden in a brake of willows, unable to fight back against Jim Randle's fusillade.

"Come on, Randle!" shouted the U. P. speculator, spurring toward the east again. "I've got what I came for. Now it doesn't matter if Preston is alive or in hell! He won't dare come back to Wagonwheel City!"

XXVI

REWARD, DEAD OR ALIVE

DELIVAN'S gleeful, mocking words rang in Preston's ears as the cowboy watched the speculator and his bodyguard dwindle in the distance toward the east end of the pass.

"There goes Delivan and my ace in the hole—"

Preston knew, without riding back to the site of his destroyed cabin, that the homestead documents he had been in the act of digging out of their cache were gone.

There was nothing he could do to prevent their theft, not so long as Delivan and his partner were armed with long-range rifles. To buck them with the six-guns he had borrowed at the survey camp would be suicidal.

Sick at heart, the Texan emerged from hiding and rode Alamo back across the river. Once more he stood beside the blue gypsum boulder which was Panhandle Preston's tombstone. His eyes filled as he addressed the oblong mound:

"Delivan ain't got us licked, dad. He thinks I dassn't show up in Wagonwheel City, now that I'm a wanted hombre. But that's where Delivan's wrong."

He headed back toward the forest-choked end of Tomahawk Pass at a ground-covering lope that would spare himself and horse. There was no use trying to overtake Delivan; showdown must come at Wagonwheel City.

He avoided Gorine's camp by taking the north trail where a few days before the boss surveyor had captured him with Weldon. Delivan had no doubt tipped off the surveyors that he, Preston, was an escaped fugitive from military justice. While Preston had reason to believe the engineers were friendly, it would not pay to take chances on their seeing their duty and arresting him.

The surveyors, the night before, had dressed his wounds and given him supper and breakfast this morning. His weariness had been wiped out by the long sleep he had enjoyed in Gorine's tent. He had informed them of the major's death, giving them what scant details Helen had told him; but regarding his own court-martial he had remained prudently silent.

The forty-mile ride across the open plains east of the Sioux Bonnets was packed with suspense for the cowboy. He dared not take the easy route and follow the U. P. tracks to town, for fear of being sighted by soldiers or Irish track workers.

The northerly route was dangerous because of the Sioux he knew to be infesting the region, concentrating for one last desperate offensive against the encroaching Iron Horse.

He saw lone scouts on hill crests, looking out over the trail of the Iron Horse; once, far in the distance, he sighted the tepees of a big Sioux camp.

But nightfall found Preston sitting his horse on the ridge overlooking Wagonwheel Springs once more, at the selfsame spot where he and his father—was it an eternity ago?—had first glimpsed the teeming confusion below.

The town had diminished appreciably in size since that morning; the cavalry barracks were more than half dismantled, to be moved thirty miles westward to end-of-track. But somewhere down there would be Boone Delivan, smug in the belief that he had cheated Preston out of his Tomahawk Pass right-of-way.

Preston knew, with a bitter despair in his heart, that he could never claim the Lone Star Ranch again as long as the taint of murder was on his good name. But his flaming six-guns would make sure that Boone Delivan did not harvest his ill-gotten gains, before another sun had risen.

Somewhere down there, too, would be Helen Gorine; and Quent was conscious of an overpowering desire to see the girl again, and make sure that she had suffered no serious hurts from yesterday morning's train wreck.

He waited in the undergrowth until darkness had deepened into indigo over the flats. Then he rode down the slope and tied Alamo to a fence rail, making his way on foot toward the main street.

In the shelter of a black alleyway alongside the Red Tent Saloon he stripped off his telltale Texas chaps and stuffed them under the barroom foundations. There was no use advertising the fact he was a cowpuncher.

A quarter-inch growth of black stubble disguised his face.

Adjusting the bulk of his thonged-down Colts, Quent Preston emerged into the lamplighted main stem. He saw a light in Ellis Bayard's office, and the blood raced hotly within him.

After his showdown with Boone Delivan, Preston would pay a lethal visit to the lawyer's shack, also. It had been Bayard's perjured evidence at the court-martial that had convicted Preston of the murder of Lige Morton. Bayard, before he died, would cast some light on the true facts about the marshal's death.

The revenge-lusting heart of a ruthless killer throbbed within Preston as he followed the foot traffic, eyes shuttling from face to face, hunting Delivan's.

A uniformed aide-de-camp from Colonel Sires' headquarters brushed past Preston, a sheaf of cardboard placards under one elbow. He tacked one of the signs to the supporting post of a wooden awning in front of a gambling den, and went on.

Light from the lobby windows of the big End-of-Track Hotel illuminated the sign. Quent

Preston stiffened as he saw his own name glaring at him from big red letters:

$1,000 REWARD, DEAD OR ALIVE
will be paid for the capture
of a fugitive from military
prison known as
QUENT PRESTON
Convicted of murder; escaped
from U. P. jail train wrecked west
of here by the Indians!

There followed, in smaller type, a fairly complete description of himself and of Alamo, his claybank mount.

Men crowded about him to read the sign. The cowboy's neck nape prickled as he heard the reaction of the uncouth spectators:

"That thousand simoleons would come in handy, eh, Tom?"

"Preston won't hang around these parts, though."

"Hell, no. If the Injuns don't ketch him, he'll light a shuck for Californy, prob'ly."

Preston elbowed his way into darker shadows, keeping his Stetson brim pulled low to shield his face from the scrutiny of passers-by. Then he heard a familiar voice above the din of traffic:

"This way, Helen. We'll take a short cut to the house. Keep as close to Mrs. Sires as you can."

193

Preston's heart bounded within him as he caught sight of three mounted riders turning off the main street into an alley.

Colonel Sires, one arm in a sling, rode ahead. Close behind were two women—the colonel's wife, the other Helen Gorine!

Except that her face was paler than usual, the girl showed no signs of injury. Her face was impassive, expressionless as she rode within a dozen feet of the spot where Preston stood in the shadows, shoulder-blades pressed against a blacksmith-shop wall.

A wild desire to rush out and greet the girl surged through Preston's veins, but he restrained his feelings until they had passed. Then he skulked after them, jostling men who were heading for the main street.

He saw Colonel Sires and the two women cross the Union Pacific tracks and head for a frame dwelling house near the cavalry grounds. A uniformed attendant took the reins of their horses, and then Colonel Sires escorted the women inside.

"Helen's stopping with Colonel Sires' family, I reckon," concluded the Texan, a surge of relief going through his being. "Leastwise, I'll know she's in good hands."

His jaw hardened as he turned back toward town, his hands coiled about the stocks of his Colt .45s. Then an impulse stronger than his

194

primitive hate and desire for revenge impelled him to turn back toward Sires' home.

Lamplight glowed from the windows of the house. Helen was inside. Doubtlessly she would be wondering if he were alive or dead, a victim of the Indians or of injuries from the train wreck.

"I've got to let her know—some way—"

His better sense told him to beware, but Preston headed over the railroad yards in the darkness and circled about to approach Colonel Sires' home from the rear.

A sentry was pacing up and down the colonel's front porch, a rifle on his shoulder. But the rear of the house was unguarded.

Preston crawled up to a lighted window. The sash was up, and from within came the sound of women's voices:

"We'll do our best to make you comfortable, Miss Gorine. Feel welcome to remain with us until you are ready to go East."

"How can I thank you, Mrs. Sires? But I . . . I cannot go East. I have no one back there—I have no one—anywhere."

"But, my dear, poor girl—you cannot remain here on the frontier, now that your father is gone. End-of-track is no place for a sweet girl to be."

Preston's pulses hammered his eardrums as he rested his fingertips on the window ledge and peered through gauze curtains. It was a bedroom, and Helen Gorine was brushing her hair before a

195

dresser mirror. Mrs. Sires hovered at her side, her motherly face lined with anxiety.

"I am a frontier girl, Mrs. Sires," Helen replied listlessly. "But—if you will excuse me now—my father's funeral put me so on edge—perhaps tomorrow I can make some plans—"

"Of course, darling. Good night!"

Mrs. Sires kissed her and left the room. Helen Gorine turned back to her mirror—and then stiffened in alarm as she caught sight of a face in the window behind her.

She whirled about with a low cry—and then rushed to the window as she recognized Quent Preston's gaunt face.

"Oh, Quent, Quent—I'm so glad to know you're alive—"

Their hands met and clung, as Preston glanced apprehensively up and down the wall of the house. In the soft glow of lamplight he stood revealed to any possible watcher from the grounds.

"I can't stay—but I had to see you—before I leave Wagonwheel City, Helen," he whispered emotionally. "I had to see for myself—that you got out of that wreck O. K."

"But—where are you going, Quent?" Her voice was tragic.

Preston shrugged bitterly.

"*Quién Sabe?* I can use a gun and ride average well. I can get a job hunting buffalo for the U. P. track gangs, maybe."

"But they've got out a reward for you, Quent—"

"I know. But out on the far ranges, in a hunting camp, I wouldn't be known. I'll change my name. I'll get another horse, different clothes."

The girl turned from the window to blow out her lamp. Then she returned to Preston, and in the darkness she heard him gasp and circle her with buckskin-clad arms, drawing her lips to his.

"I love you, Helen," he whispered above the tom-tomming of his heart, releasing her. "Reckon—I'm a fool to be making this kind of talk, seeing as how I'm a hunted man now—but—"

Her lips found his, sending an electric thrill through him, making him forgetful of all else about him.

"Quent, dear," she breathed, her cheeks wet as she pressed her head against his. "We're both alone now—my heart will break if you leave me here. Can't we go away somewhere—away from the U. P.—and—"

Slogging boots on the hard earth along the house wall made the two break apart, Preston plummeting a hand to his Colt stock. Then he froze, as he saw the army sentinel holding him under the drop of his rifle.

"Hands up!" snarled the soldier as Helen Gorine drew back in horror. "Miss, if this drunken barfly is molesting you, I'll have him clapped in the calaboose—"

Swallowing her fear, Helen Gorine leaned from the window and said reassuringly, her voice steady:

"This isn't a drunk, Mr. Jennings. He . . . he is a friend of my father's—who attended the funeral today. He just wanted to see—if I needed anything. That was all! You may go."

The guard lowered his rifle and saluted, an apologetic smile making his teeth flash in the starlight.

"Beg pardon, miss," said the soldier, clicking his heels together and shouldering his carbine. "But when I saw a man at your window, naturally I—well, I apologize to you, sir."

Quent Preston closed his eyes in profound relief.

"That . . . that's all right, feller," he managed to say. "You were just doing your duty. I reckon I'll take a pasear over to camp now, Miss Gorine. *Buenos noches—*"

As Preston stepped away he felt a six-gun jam against his spine and a harsh voice said against his ear:

"I'm sorry, Preston. I'm sorry for you, too, Helen. But I had rather expected Preston might be foolhardy enough to try to visit you, instead of leaving Wyoming."

The startled guard saw Quent Preston turn about, to face the silhouetted figure of Colonel Sires, who had approached from around the corner of the house.

Starlight glittered on the military pistol which the army man held against the cowboy's ribs.

"This time, Helen will not rescue you from the firing squad," clipped Sires in a steely voice. "Private Jennings, disarm this man and conduct him to jail. Put him under *triple* guard!"

XXVII

TRAPPED

HELEN GORINE placed a boot toe on the window sill before her as she saw the army sentinel step forward to take Quent Preston into custody.

The cowboy glanced up with despair-glazed eyes as he lowered his arms to receive the sentry's heavy army handcuffs, and, as he did so, Preston saw the girl lift her other foot to balance herself on the ledge of the window.

Grim light blazed in the girl's eyes. She was no gently bred woman softened by civilization, but a whip-muscled creature of the frontier, hardened by years of outdoor living and with her blood afire with the reckless courage a frontier woman would feel when fighting in defense of the man she loved.

Even as Colonel Sires reached for the buttoned flap of his cavalry holster to return his six-gun to its scabbard, Helen Gorine leaped down upon the old war dog's shoulders.

With a grunt of surprise the army commander sprawled to the ground, Helen's arms wrapped in a smothering embrace about his neck.

"Hurry—Quent—"

But the Texan had gone into action the very

instant he had seen Helen Gorine launch her dive at the unsuspecting army colonel.

Even as the sentry grounded the butt of his rifle and drew his handcuffs from a uniform pocket, Quent Preston's right fist came up in a smoking uppercut which snapped the sentry's head back on his shoulders.

A swift-following left to the pit of the stomach doubled up the soldier and dropped him groaning, fingers dropping the handcuffs.

With a savage oath, Colonel Sires flung Helen's bulk away from him and sought to jerk up his still unholstered gun. But Quent Preston had no intention of remaining a target within the range of the colonel's weapon.

Snatching up the soldier's rifle, the cowboy hurled it through the window of Helen's bedroom and vaulted over the sill after it.

Rearing to his feet, Colonel Sires pushed Helen Gorine aside and triggered three fast shots into the room, but Quent Preston was scuttling on hands and knees across the bedroom floor, safely below the colonel's line of fire.

A peal of hysterical laughter came from the girl as she saw the colonel shrink back from the open window, afraid to climb in after the escaping cowboy for fear of stopping a bullet from the rifle which Preston had taken with him.

Off to one side, the half-dazed sentry was picking himself out of the dust, feeling his jaw with trembling fingers and shaking his head to clear it.

"I'll court-martial you for this, Helen!" raged the army commander, his eyes blazing as he whirled to face the girl who had hurled herself upon him. "If Preston makes his getaway, by the gods I'll see you rot in jail, woman or not!"

Inside the bedroom, Quent Preston fumbled for a corridor doorknob, his ears registering the army colonel's furious tirade and Helen Gorine's defiant laughter. Then the night air resounded to Sires' yells, as running footsteps told of the approach of soldiers from nearby barracks.

"I'd be trapped like a skunk in a barrel if I stay in this house," panted the Texan, finding the doorknob and opening the door. "Sires'll have this place surrounded in another couple of ticks—"

The doorway opened on the hall through which he had seen the colonel's wife depart a few minutes before. At the far end light glowed through the cracks of a living-room door. At the opposite end was a glass-paneled door opening on a rear porch.

Making sure that his army rifle was loaded, Quent Preston fled toward the porch door. Then, even as he reached for the knob, he saw the figure of Colonel Sires and another soldier racing up outside.

"He can't get out—watch this door, Bert!"

ordered the army man. "We'll smoke him out of here if we have to burn down my house—"

Preston found another door in the flimsy partition, pried the lock, and admitted himself into a dark room which, from the odor of food, was apparently a storage room or pantry.

A single window showed stars outside; it was open, and the cool night breeze whipped Preston's face as he groped in the darkness until he came to the outer wall.

A quick look up and down the outside revealed that as yet no sentry was posted on this flank of the house. Quickly Preston swung out the window and dropped to the ground, whipping the army rifle to his shoulder and standing at rigid attention as he heard Colonel Sires racing around the nearby corner, saber clanking in its scabbard.

"Keep your post, Maddux!" roared the officer, plainly mistaking Preston for one of his house sentries in the darkness. "That damned fugitive, Preston, is loose inside. If he tries getting out any of these windows, shoot first and ask questions afterward!"

Preston mumbled a gruff "Yes, sir!" in his best army fashion, as the panting officer raced on around the building to continue giving orders for the surrounding of the house.

He had a moment's respite in which to recover his breath, but to remain here would be fatal. It would be but a matter of seconds before Colonel

Sires would undoubtedly bump into Maddux, the sentinel whose duty it was to patrol this side of the building.

Then Sires would discover his mistake in identity, and order his soldiers to open fire.

Sucking in a deep breath, Quent Preston headed out into the starlight at a run, making in the direction of Wagonwheel. Not until he had crossed the U. P. tracks and gained the refuge of the boom town's hundreds of tents and dark lanes would he be safe.

An ear-shattering roar of gunnery blasted the night and bullets whistled on all sides of him as he gained the middle of the parade grounds.

With a panicked gasp, Preston realized that already he had been discovered making his flight.

"It's Preston!" came Colonel Sires' bullish roar out of the night.

Cavalrymen were swarming out of barracks behind Sires' house. Soldiers were snapping guns to their shoulders and taking pot shots at the fleeing cowboy out in the deserted parade ground, a zigzagging ghost against the background of the tented city.

A bullet scathed Preston's thigh, the shock of it dropping him to his knees. He picked himself up and staggered on, then whirled and aimed his rifle in the general direction of Sires' house, intending to answer the pelting gunfire with a shot which might make his foemen scatter to cover.

But the trigger mechanism of the army rifle jammed under the pressure of Preston's finger. In his fall the gun breech must have become fouled with grit and dirt.

Throwing the useless weapon aside with a despairing curse, Preston headed toward the nearest barracks. With a dozen or more riflemen concentrating their fire on him, it was doubtful if he could reach the shelter of Wagonwheel City.

He sprang up the steps of the deserted barracks and knocked in the door lock with the terrific drive of catapulting shoulders. His breath whistled with relief as he saw that the building was an armory, empty of soldiers.

Gasping for breath, Preston slammed shut the door and struck a match. Racked guns, kegs of powder, and bales of army uniforms were on all sides. He found a heavy steel bar from a cannon mount and barricaded the damaged door lock, then struck another match and peered about him.

The armory shack was without windows—a factor slightly in his favor, for he knew he would be promptly surrounded.

"Reckon I was loco for dodging in here," panted the Texan, kneeling beside the door and putting his ear to the keyhole. "But I'd have been tallied for sure, out there in the open—"

Slogging army boots were crossing the drill ground. Colonel Sires' hoarse voice was bawling orders. A platoon or more of cavalry, roused from their barracks by the sound of yells and gunshots, were racing across the grounds toward the armory shack which he had chosen for a shelter.

Already he was surrounded. A tight ring of soldiery had been flung about the armory, and above the thud of boots and the yells of excited men Preston heard Sires' voice roar out:

"Open that door and come out with your hands up, Preston! You haven't got a chance!"

Preston crawled along the floor until he butted up against a keg of gunpowder. He paused, groping about in the hopes of finding a case of ammunition for the racks of army rifles he had seen along the walls.

Then an idea burst upon his consciousness, as he remembered the bales of dark-blue army uniforms which were stored in the room beside him.

Crawling through the blackness, he came upon one of the bundles. With steady fingers he unbuckled the straps binding one of the bales of clothing, and his groping hands lifted up a cavalryman's brass-buttoned coat.

Moving with feverish haste in the darkness, Preston wriggled into the loose-fitting army coat and buttoned it up. Then he removed his Levis and replaced them with the coarse blue woolen trousers with the vivid yellow stripe of Battalion K, United States Cavalry.

Thus garbed, Preston crawled along the floor to

the far end of the armory. The yells had subsided outdoors, but the Texan's acute ears heard the low voices of cavalrymen who had surrounded the building.

Again came Colonel Sires' harsh order from the front door:

"We'll give you ten seconds to surrender, Preston, and then we'll break in this door!"

Preston drew a deep breath, flattened himself on the floor, and shouted back:

"Ain't you forgetting, Sires, that I've got plenty of army guns to fight back with, if you do come in?"

Sires retorted sarcastically:

"That's a bluff, Preston. You've got plenty of rifles, yes—but they're all unloaded, and all the rifle ammunition was moved out of there and shipped to end-of-track only this morning!"

Preston crept out into midfloor, taking no chances on a guard locating his voice and firing through the flimsy clapboard walls.

"Try breaking in, Sires, and I'll set fire to this gunpowder and blow the whole U. S. army to hell!"

There was a moment's confusion outside. Then Colonel Sires' voice rang out in a command to his men:

"The fool might try to break open a keg of powder and wreck the armory at that, men. Stand by while we knock in this door!"

Preston leaped to his feet and tiptoed to the spot on the wall near the door where he had seen the racked carbines. He took one off the rack and shouldered it, at the same time pressing himself back against the dark wall.

There was a series of splintering crashes and men's grunting voices, as Sires ordered the door broken down. The steel bar under the knob held, but not so the wooden panels of the door itself.

A moment later, Preston saw the door smash inward to admit six burly-shouldered cavalrymen, starlight throwing them in sinister outline in the doorway.

XXVIII

A BUFFALO HUNTER

H E'S unarmed—take him!" yelled Colonel Sires, pushing through the men who hesitated in the doorway. "Bring a light, somebody!"

Quent Preston moved nearer the broken doorway, as the cavalrymen pushed through into the armory, eyes searching the dense blackness for a trace of the cowboy they believed to be cowering somewhere in the far end of the room.

A match flared as a beefy sergeant struck a light and peered about. The room was filling with blue-uniformed men, most of them hatless and disheveled from having just come from the barracks.

Therefore, fleeting glances paid no concern to Quent Preston, passing up the blue-uniformed cowboy without interest as they scanned the piled-up boxes and bales in the armory room.

"Only place he could be hiding is over behind those gunpowder kegs!" snapped Colonel Sires, leading the way toward the far end of the armory. "Don't worry about him setting off an explosion—those kegs are hard to break open. The instant you see a match, shoot!"

The match in the sergeant's fingers died off, and the soldiers spread apart in the gloom as they started an advance down the armory floor toward the corner which, as Sires had said, offered the only possible hiding place for a man.

Other cavalrymen brushed past Quent Preston to get inside, one of them carrying a lighted army lantern from the barracks. In their haste to gain Colonel Sires' side, the man with the lantern paid no notice to the uniformed Texan beside the door, assuming that he was a sentry posted there to prevent any possible attempt on Preston's part to bolt for freedom.

Calmly stepping over the wreckage of the armory door, Quent Preston walked out into the cool night. Inside the armory he saw the excited cavalrymen backing Colonel Sires as the purple-visaged old soldier, with drawn six-gun, cautiously approached the pile of boxes and powder kegs behind which they were positive their quarry was hiding.

Moving unhurriedly, Preston shouldered his rifle in army style and marched toward the nearby U. P. tracks. Beyond them lay Wagonwheel City and safety.

He was in the act of stepping over the steel rails when loud shouts and the rumble of boots inside the armory told the cowboy that his escape had been confirmed. No doubt, the discovery of an opened bundle of army uniforms, and Preston's own overalls, had told Colonel Sires their own story of Preston's disguise.

Tossing aside the useless army gun—closer inspection had revealed the fact that the rifle he had removed from the army rack did not even have a bolt—Quent Preston broke into a run and vanished into the tent-lined lanes of Wagonwheel City.

Behind him, like wolfhounds baying on the scent of prey, came the United States cavalrymen. Although they had nothing to go by, they were coming directly after him, knowing that Preston would undoubtedly head for the construction camp.

"They'll be madder'n wet hens, too," chuckled Preston, not unaware of the humor of his getaway. "Reckon they'll open fire on anything they see ramblin' around loose with an army outfit on. So I got to take care of that."

He ducked into a lamplighted tent, whipping the flies shut behind him, to stand blinking into a kerosene lamp placed on a table formed of a rough packing case.

A grizzled oldster with the pouchy eyes and caved-in cheeks of a saloon barfly was playing solitaire on the packing case, seated on a crude cot which formed the tent's only other furniture.

"What yuh want, soldier?" demanded the startled derelict, half rising. "Bustin' in a man's tent thataway—I ain't done—"

Preston reached inside the army coat to fumble in the pocket of his own shirt. He drew forth a crumpled bank note and dropped it on the oldster's solitaire layout.

"Twenty bucks I'm offering you for that Stetson you're wearing and them overalls yonder," said Preston tersely. "They ain't worth five, but the twenty's yours."

The barfly's eyes slitted greedily as he surveyed Preston's tousled hair and ill-fitting army uniform.

"Desertin', eh?" wheezed the drunkard. "Want to git out of your uniform, eh? Well, twenty bucks wouldn't buy the band offn my John B., soldier. It'll cost ye—"

Excited yells of hard-running cavalrymen beyond the tent's walls made Preston desperate. Whipping off his uniform coat, the cowboy slapped it about the ancient drunkard's head like a hood before the barfly was aware of what was happening.

Wadding the coat fabric into the barfly's toothless jaws, Preston wrapped the sleeves tightly about the oldster's head, knotting them in place to form a gag.

Then, pinning the oldster flat on the cot with one knee, the cowboy snatched up a bit of tent rope and knotted the barfly's wrists to his ankles.

"Hated like hell to rumple you up, old-timer," panted Quent Preston as he picked up the barfly's untidy blue beaver Stetson and clapped it on his own head. "But I'm leaving you that twenty dollars. You'll be loose of that gag in ten minutes, and able to bellow for help. Then you can buy a new hat—or redeye whiskey—or anything you please."

Preston peeled off the army trousers and got into the drunkard's multipatched bib overalls.

Then, blowing out the oldster's lamp, Preston ducked out the tent door and walked swiftly toward the main street.

The clothing he had appropriated by force was ancient and practically worthless, but it would serve him in good stead tonight, for it made him inconspicuous and shoddy-looking, similar to any one of a thousand nondescript, fate-tossed outcasts common to the boom camps of the U. P. R.

"One thing certain, I got to get out of Wagonwheel tonight," panted Quent, as he headed toward the spot where he had left Alamo. "With the whole town knowing I'm on the loose, Boone Delivan would be all primed and waiting for me to show up."

In the alley alongside the Red Tent Saloon he paused to recover his Texas chaps. A few minutes later found him tightening the girth on Alamo's saddle.

A sense of bitterness and frustration consumed the Texan a quarter hour later when he drew rein atop the hill overlooking Wagonwheel City.

The twinkling lights of the construction camp in the darkness below seemed to mock him. Boone Delivan was somewhere down there, momentarily secure from revenge. But the thought that Helen Gorine was down there also, praying for his safety, was soothing to Preston's dejected spirits.

"*Hasta luego,* Helen!" the Texan called down into the darkness, as he wheeled Alamo to the northward. "I'm wondering if we'll ever be meetin' again—"

He spurred off through the black lodgepole pines which he and his father had explored so often in the past. A consuming sense of loneliness filled him as he headed northward into the menacing hills of the Sioux country.

Like the Indians, he was now marked quarry for army bullets. But unlike the Sioux, Preston was traveling a lone-wolf trail, one man pitted against all other men and against the perilous wild lands.

Had he not strayed off trail tonight, to see Helen Gorine, he would have fulfilled his vengeance against Boone Delivan by now. But the memory of the girl's kisses filled him with a sense of peace.

Alamo, tireless and foot-sure, covered fifty miles of broken country before dawn broke. Yet Preston pushed on, knowing the danger of being caught, hungry and unarmed, in the heart of the Sioux country.

The red men, making their last, desperate, back-to-the-wall stand against the Union Pacific and all it represented, would run down any white man they encountered in the wilds. And, from what Preston had been able to gather from hearsay and his own knowledge of the Sioux, he believed that the badlands within one hundred miles of the U. P. trail were swarming with warriors.

Luck was with him at midmorning when, gaunt from fatigue and with his stomach racked with hunger, he came across a lonely sod-roofed cabin that had belonged, no doubt, to a trapper. It showed signs of having been abandoned hastily, the owner probably having spotted Indian sign and realized it would be safest to take his pelts and head for safer country.

At any rate, there were bags of parched corn and jerked buffalo meat hanging from the rafters of the shack, and clear water in a spring nearby, with grass for Alamo.

Preston built a fire in the crude hearth, which reminded him, with a pang, of the cabin he and Panhandle had built in Tomahawk Pass and which was now an ash heap.

After he had cooked a meal and loaded the abandoned food supplies aboard his saddle, Preston headed off toward the eastward, the westering sun at his back. He hated to leave the cool spring and the sanctuary of the cabin, but he knew a white man's house would draw Indians like flies to a honey pot.

Once, in late afternoon, he spotted a moving dust which he mistook for a large band of Sioux; and went into hiding. But the dark blot on the prairie resolved itself into a herd of buffalo.

He camped that night on the east bank of the Big Sandy River. Another day of travel would put him out of the Sioux territory; he had provisions enough to get him to Fort Laramie, where he might be able to get work with a wagon freighter or at a livery outfit.

He slept the sleep of healthy exhaustion that night, his jagged nerves soothed by the gentle swish of the Big Sandy's ripples over its gravelly bed.

The sun was an hour high, next morning, when Preston was shocked out of profound slumber by the shadow of a horse and rider falling across his face.

Terror jelled the Texan's blood as he clutched hands instinctively to his thighs, feeling for guns that were not there.

His eyes focused on the muddy hoofs and fetlocks of an Indian pony, and his gaze traveled upward, fully expecting to see a leering Sioux poised with tomahawk or rifle above him.

Instead, he saw a yellow-bearded American in a buffalo-hide coat balancing a mighty Sharps rifle across his saddle pommel. The rider grunted and hipped over in saddle as Preston bounded to his feet, muscles sore from his long sleep with only a saddle blanket for bedding.

"Howdy, stranger," greeted the bearded horseman. "A mite risky, ain't it, beddin' down in Injun country with no shootin' irons around?"

Preston relaxed, sensing no hostility in the other's tone.

"Been dodgin' Injuns for days," he responded, pointing to the bloodstains on his shirt. "This is where I pulled a Sioux arrow out of my skin."

"What you doin' out here so far from nowhere?"

"My ranch was burned out. I was lucky to get away with my clothes and my horse."

Preston did not see fit to explain the actual circumstances of his ranch fire, letting this stranger assume he had been the victim of an Indian attack. He had not yet given his name, nor did the big stranger appear curious. It was doubtful, Preston realized, whether this plainsman had heard of him, let alone the one-thousand-dollar reward posted for his capture at Wagonwheel City.

"Right nice hossflesh you're forking, stranger," commented the flaxen-bearded rider. "From Texas, ain't you?"

"That's right."

"That means you can handle guns and a hoss and a rope?"

217

"If I couldn't, I wouldn't be here. Reckon I've saved my hair with all three of the things you mentioned."

The bearded rider dismounted and extended a hand.

"I'm Bighorn Ben Kettenring," introduced the grizzled one. "I got a contract to keep the U. P. R. in buffalo meat, and I'm short of hunters. How'd you like a job shootin' buffalo, son?"

Quent Preston's heart leaped. A job in a buffalo camp would keep him far from the railroad, far from reward-hunting cavalrymen, far from the menace of Boone Delivan's gun hawks. It would give him a chance to grow a beard to disguise himself, recover his outlook on life and restore his jaded body.

"Bighorn, you've hired yourself a hand," said Quent Preston. "My name's Quentin—sometimes known as Texas Slim."

XXIX

TEXAS SLIM, ACE HUNTER

THE next three weeks were adventure-packed ones for Texas Slim, as Preston became known in Kettenring's buffalo camp. There was the ever-present threat of Indian attack, for Kettenring and his huntsmen were engaged in the task of stripping the Sioux hunting grounds of their buffalo, and, as such, were the most hated of all whites.

There were seven men, all experts with high-powered rifles, in Kettenring's camp. Rough, coarse-tongued men, with shaggy beards and flintlike eyes; and all were noncommittal about their pasts, a factor which Quent Preston found to his liking, for he asked no questions and had to answer none.

Every day's work began an hour before sunup, to give the riders time to get out to bedded-down herds of bison. Each hunter was supposed to pick his game with care, killing only yearlings whose meat would be tender, and sparing cows with suckling calves at their sides.

At times, the big bulls who led the small herds would delay a stampede to attack a hunter whose thundering rifle had brought down a buffalo, in which case it was necessary to slay the bull. But in the latter event, the bull's hide was skinned off and the carcass left for the scavenging coyotes and buzzards. Quent Preston's lifetime in the saddle, spent down in Texas in the hazardous work of herding Panhandle longhorns up long cattle trails, made the cowboy ideally fitted for buffalo hunting.

Because of the skill of the claybank peg pony between his knees, responding instantly to spoken commands, the pressure of knees or the light touch of spur or rein, Preston was able to bag more than his share of prime buffalo during each day's work.

As a result, he was soon aware of a sullen jealousy on the part of the other men in Kettenring's bunch. But he was paid well, and the blond giant who paid him was well satisfied with his new hand.

"You better throw in your chips with me, after this Union Pacific contract is finished, Slim," advised Kettenring, one night at a campfire where they were waiting for Kettenring's big freight wagons to arrive from Wagonwheel City, to transport freshly butchered meat to rail. "I got a contract to furnish meat to the army outpost at Laramie, an' I'll probably have it for years to come. We could clean up."

Preston, staring moodily into the fire, shook his head gloomily.

"Shooting buffalo don't appeal to me,

Kettenring," he said frankly. "I sort of feel like I'm playing a scurvy trick on the Indians who really own them buffalo."

The other hunters grunted in astonishment. To them, a Sioux was only a varmint, to be shot at sight like a marauding wolf.

"That's funny talk to be comin' from a feller that almost lost his ha'r to an Injun," grunted Kettenring.

Preston stirred impatiently, his hands idly fingering his six-gun holsters, six-guns which he had been furnished by Kettenring and the cost of which had been taken out of his first week's pay.

"It's the waste, too," went on Preston, waving a hand toward the piles of butchered meat covered by tarpaulins a few feet away, awaiting delivery to railhead. "We've shot fifty tons of buffalo this past week, and only the choicest steaks are being used. The rate we're going, and the other buffalo hunters in this country, there won't be any buffalo left for the Injuns or anyone else."

Kettenring grunted in his yellow beard, his eyes studying his new hunter quizzically.

"When the buffalo are gone, thar'll be other ways to make a livin'," retorted the boss hunter. "You're makin' a new stake, ain't you? What are you complainin' about?"

Quent Preston lifted his gaze across the crackling campfire to study the flushed Teutonic face of Kettenring. He knew the big hunter could

221

never fathom a true Westerner's way of looking at things. To Kettenring, the annihilation of the American bison was in the run of business. The West was a horn of plenty to be tapped and drained and left barren and empty.

"I ain't complaining, Kettenring," answered the Texan. "I'm just telling you I don't hanker to be your pardner after this U. P. contract is up. I just can't stomach this waste of meat and—"

A sharp whistle from a sentinel rider out in the darkness made the hunters leap to their feet, guns ready against the chance that the lookout had spotted Indians.

"The wagons are comin'!" came the cry of the sentinel.

Quent Preston lifted a hand to his face. His cheeks and jaw were covered with an inch of soft brown beard, now, so that he had no fear of being recognized by any of the freighters from Wagonwheel City.

A few minutes later the big canvas-hooded freight wagons lumbered into camp. Once a week they visited the hunting grounds, loading fresh meat into the heavy wagon beds and returning to the Union Pacific boom camp.

There were loud greetings from the incoming muleskinners, as wagons were unhitched. Tobacco and canned food were dumped beside the campfire to replenish Kettenring's supplies; and on every tongue was range gossip about the

U. P. and Indian scares and the latest shootings at Wagonwheel City.

After the excitement of the arrival of the wagons had diminished and men were beginning to seek out their buffalo-robe bedrolls, Quent Preston found a copy of the Wagonwheel City *Gazette* of the previous week, serving as a wrapper for a bundle of woolen socks ordered by Kettenring's hunters.

On the front page, surrounded by a heavy black rule, was the one-thousand-dollar reward notice for his own capture. The type was beginning to get clogged with lint, showing that it was running from week to week in the paper.

The main headline caught Preston's eyes and made him wince in spite of himself:

UNION PACIFIC NOW BUILDING
THROUGH TOMAHAWK PASS AS
BOONE DELIVAN SELLS A
RIGHT-OF-WAY STRIP

The story below the headline was pregnant with interest for the bearded cowboy as he read it by the light of the flickering campfire:

The Irish paddies of the U. P. R. are now engaged in laying track and building trestles through Tomahawk Pass, end-of-track now being fifty miles west from Wagonwheel City.

General Dodge is on hand and is loud in his praise of the engineering genius of the late Major John Gorine, who ran the survey through the Pass.

The last barrier to the U. P. R. was removed this week when a right-of-way deal through the Pass was made between the Union Pacific and Mr. Boone Delivan, recent purchaser of the Tomahawk Pass area. Delivan is reported to have sold the right-of-way for $40,000, a figure considerably less than his first offer.

"I do not wish to stand in the way of the progress of the Union Pacific," Delivan told the *Gazette* editor as we went to press. "Rather than tie up the railroad with a lawsuit, I am sacrificing my property in Tomahawk Pass."

The news left Quent Preston limp and gray, his eyes staring bitterly at the single-sheet newspaper.

Boone Delivan's triumph was complete; he had acquired title to the Lone Star Ranch, doubtlessly through forged papers drawn up by the unscrupulous lawyer, Ellis Bayard, with the help of the deeds which he had stolen from Preston's ranchhouse.

Preston got to his feet and paced off into the darkness, to get control of his seething emotions. He was filled with a grim yearning to saddle up

Alamo and ride to Wagonwheel, there to complete his vengeance against Boone Delivan.

It was, he realized, too late to save the homestead which he and his father had developed in Tomahawk Pass. But a savage desire to slay the man who had defrauded him made Preston's blood burn, made his heart slam his ribs.

But a tempering emotion urged him to lie low here in Kettenring's buffalo camp, where he would be secure from reward hunters. He was making money at honest, though distasteful work; he now had guns, new boots, sturdy clothing.

When he had escaped from Wagonwheel City three weeks before, his horizon had been confined to the limits of inflicting vengeance upon Boone Delivan, the author of his outcast misery.

But in the ensuing days, the memory of Helen Gorine's offer to share his perilous existence had given him a deeper purpose in life, one which he wanted to protect and not risk by a foolhardy visit to Wagonwheel.

Quent was beginning to realize that the fullness of his manhood was not to be wasted or lost, merely because Tomahawk Pass and all he and his father had known and loved and worked for was lost beyond hope of recovery.

"Damned if I won't play out my string here with Kettenring until the Union Pacific is finished," Quent thought as he turned back toward the camp. "There'll be plenty of time to track down Boone Delivan. It's up to me to make a stake so I can offer Helen a life that'll be better than tying up with a hunted man. We can go somewhere else and make a fresh start—maybe down in Texas somewhere—"

Bighorn Ben Kettenring was squatting beside the campfire talking to the boss of the wagon string when Preston returned into the firelight. At sound of Preston's boots, Kettenring turned about and said:

"Randle here needs a wagon scout to watch for Injuns on the way back to Wagonwheel City, Slim. I reckon you're the man for the job, seein' as how you shoot and ride like a top hand, and you seem to know the country."

The sombreroed wagon-train boss nodded.

"Seen plenty of Injun sign on this trip. Wouldn't be surprised if we weren't attacked before we get back to—"

The wagon boss broke off, as he looked up to study Quent Preston's face in the firelight. At the same instant, Preston got his first full view of the wagoneer's countenance, and a tug of recognition made his face blanch.

Somewhere, sometime, he had seen this man Randle before. The quality of the man's harsh, guttural voice was familiar in his ears.

Then, with a shock of concern, Preston placed

the wagon boss' face. This man Randle was the gun hawk who had accompanied Boone Delivan to the Lone Star Ranch, and had kept Preston at bay with a .30-.30 Winchester while Delivan looted his hidden box of the government deed to the Tomahawk Pass homestead!

"What's this busky's name, Bighorn?" demanded Randle, slowly rising to his feet to face Preston.

"Texas Slim, we call him. You can take my word he'll be O.K. for a trail scout, Randle. Texas Slim can ride and shoot an'—"

Randle's palm made a slapping sound as it hit the butt of a low-slung Colt .45.

"The hell his name is Texas Slim!" snarled the wagoneer, his stubby fingers coiling about the Colt handle. "He's wanted by the army back in Wagonwheel City by the name of Quent Preston!"

Even as Randle's gun lifted from leather to gleam in the fitful firelight, the killer checked his trigger finger as he saw a Colt .45 appear magically in Preston's hand.

"Holster up, Randle," panted the Texan as he backed away to clear Kettenring from the line of fire, "or I'll kill you!"

XXX

INDIAN MASSACRE

RANDLE'S mouth drew in to a harsh line as he read the challenge in Preston's leveled gun and knew the threat in the cowboy's eyes was not bluff.

"Is that true, Slim?" demanded Bighorn Ben Kettenring, lumbering to his feet and staring aghast at his hunter. "Are you an owl-hooter with a bounty on your head?"

Quent Preston was backing slowly in the direction of his saddle and bedroll, his gun remaining fixed on Randle.

"Your wagon boss seems to think so," rasped the cowboy. "Randle, I'm countin' three. If you ain't dropped your holt on that gun by then, you'll—"

Brrrrang! Randle's left hand, hidden in shadow, plummeted to his other Colt and came up thundering. But the shot was gotten off too fast for accurate aiming, and the bullet showered gravel over Preston's boots even as the Texan pulled trigger.

With a gagged oath, Boone Delivan's gunman pitched back under the impact of a slug drilling his ribs. Ben Kettenring leaped forward, to save Randle from toppling sideways into the crackling flames.

228

Oblivious to the startled yells of the hunters and freighters who had been roused from sleep by the sudden exchange of shots, Quent Preston turned and raced for the saddle which served him for a pillow.

He seized it by the horn and sprinted out toward the remuda corral, even as Ben Kettenring dropped Randle's corpse and snatched up a buffalo rifle.

Then, as if thinking better of his impulse, Kettenring lowered the gun as Preston vanished into the outer circle of darkness.

Preston knew his margin of safety was measured by minutes now. Once the camp realized that it had harbored an outlaw with a thousand-dollar reward on his scalp, bullets would fly.

A whistle brought Alamo to the corral fence. With deft hands Preston whipped his saddle aboard the leggy claybank, hitched it frantically, and a moment later was forking the pony and spurring out into the rimming blackness of the buffalo camp.

Behind him, Preston had left grim death. Silhouetted against the guttering campfire he saw the buffalo hunters, clad in sock feet and many of them shirtless, milling around Randle's corpse. Loud voices reached his ears above the hammering of Alamo's hoofs.

And then, out of the starless Wyoming night, came the ear-splitting whoop of an Indian. It was picked up instantly by dozens of other savage throats, so that the air was filled with a soul-chilling din by the time Quent Preston had reined up his horse to listen.

Then pin points of red light flickered in a wide arc on the western side of the buffalo camp, and bullets wailed off into the night as they criss-crossed through Kettenring's wagons.

Spurring into the shelter of a rocky outcrop overlooking the campground, Quent Preston's ears caught the harsh thunder of speeding hoofs, and bare seconds later he was cut off from the camp by galloping horses, all seemingly riderless.

But the Texan knew that on the near side of each of those fleet ponies would be plastered a naked Sioux warrior.

Yells ripped the night. Kettenring's men, trapped from their bedrolls where their rifles had rested in readiness for surprise attack, were fleeing for the shelter of the wagons.

Mules brayed piteously as the encircling Indians poured volley after volley of lead in the corral. The night was hideous with the wails of wounded animals and men and the still more hideous war whoops of the attacking savages.

Realizing the danger of his own position, Quent Preston spurred up the flanking hillside until he had gained the crest of the ridge which overlooked Kettenring's camp.

Only scant moments before, painted Sioux braves had crouched behind this selfsame ridge, watching the camp below, waiting for the dawn to make their attack.

It had been the brief gun battle between Randle and Preston, the cowboy realized, that had startled the Sioux into a premature attack on the buffalo hunters. As a rule, the plains Indians made their charges in the bleak hour just before sunup, when vigilance was most lax and men's brains were drugged by sleep.

"My God," groaned the cowboy, as he tried to shut from his ears the grim noise of battle on the flats below. "I got out of there just a couple of ticks ahead of a massacre that—"

He cursed into the night as he leaned down to feel in the boot of his saddle only to realize that his own buffalo rifle lay down beside his bedroll.

It would be useless to fire on the attacking Sioux with six-guns. He was out of range, and to shoot would only betray his own position outside of the circle of doom.

Preston recalled, now, the worried conversation of the wagon drivers on their arrival that night. They had spotted Indian sign, knew they were being trailed by Sioux. Kettenring had even assigned to Preston the dangerous role of trail scout on the wagons' return trek to Wagonwheel City.

Flaming arrows zoomed upward from behind a

rock nest on the far side of the flats, looking like comets as they arched up into the heavens to fall with unerring accuracy upon the canvas hoods of the meat wagons.

From his position atop the hills, Quent Preston had a bird's-eye view of the one-sided fight below. Soon the wagon canvas was ablaze, set by the fire arrows of the Sioux.

The ruddy light picked out the ghastly forms of dead white men, slain by the first volley of Indian bullets before they could leave the vicinity of the campfire. Others had died in their beds, cut down by ruthless bullets.

Kettenring and the few hunters and mule-skinners who had gained the refuge of the wagons were shooting desperately from the wagon wheels, the pink flashes of their guns becoming fewer and fewer.

"It'll be a wipe-out," groaned Preston, racking his brain for some scheme by which he could help his fellow whites. "And there's nothing I can do but wait and watch—"

Dry grass was aflame now, fired by the arrows which an expert marksman was raining down upon the camp. The silhouetted figures of Indians were flickering back and forth between Preston and the flaming camp site, as the savages dismounted and closed in to administer the finishing touches of their raid with scalping knives and tomahawks.

One by one, the guns of the white defenders ceased firing. The inhuman cursing died off, voice by voice.

It was the strident yell of Bighorn Ben Kettenring, boss of the buffalo men, that was the last to fall on Quent Preston's sickening ears.

The cowboy watched from his vantage point, while feathered and gleaming-skinned Sioux ransacked the blazing camp, scalping knives flashing silver and crimson in the night, the savagery of their victory yells ringing in echoes off across the plains.

The red men were stamping out the bearded hunters who were decimating their supply of buffalo, upon which the Sioux had depended for generations for food. Their fight was just, this engagement one of the few they were winning in their onslaughts against the white hordes who followed the westering steel of the trail of the iron horse.

Yet Quent Preston felt nausea attack him as he realized that the white men were silenced forever, down in the camp that had been his home and his refuge for the better part of a month.

Lightning flashes cut through the scudding gray clouds that had hidden the moon and stars that night, and on the heels of clapping thunder came a warm dash of rain.

Preston withdrew into the valley beyond the ridge, lest he be trapped by the victorious Sioux on their return from the camp. Sheets of rain beat his hot face, hammered Alamo's brisket as they sought refuge in a copse of wild cedars bordering a creek.

The storm continued unabated until dawn began breaking up the blue-black clouds. The first sun rays found Quent Preston, drenched to the skin but grateful to be alive, busy tying Alamo in the thickest of the bosque.

The storm passed, a high wind sweeping the sky clean of clouds. The grass and shrubbery of the ridge before him lay clean and sparkling in the oblique light of the sunrise. The sky was enamel-blue, the earth refreshed by the night's rainfall. It seemed incredible that death and destruction lay beyond the ridge.

There was no sight or sign of Indians as far as Preston's eye could reach. No doubt they had returned to the western mountain country, following their night's attack on the wagon train they had followed up from the U. P. tracks the day before.

Shuddering in spite of himself, the Texan emerged into the open and climbed on foot to the crest of the ridge.

The camp site below him was deserted of Indian riders. A few buzzards already wheeled in the storm-cleaned heavens above.

Skidding in the fresh mud, Preston forced himself to visit Kettenring's ill-fated camp.

His eyes, used to violence and destruction as they were, recoiled to the indescribable scene about the sodden ashes of the campfire.

The wet, wilted copy of the *Gazette* which Preston had been reading was now blotched with crimson stains. Nearby lay the corpse of Randle, Boone Delivan's henchman who had so nearly plunged Quent Preston into eternity. Randle had been scalped!

The charred wreckage of the meat wagons served as tombstones for the huddled corpses of men. Nowhere was a dead Indian to be seen; if Kettenring's defenders had dropped a Sioux, his body had been taken by the departing redskins.

Preston found a shovel with a charred handle, and dug eleven graves in the shadows of the ruined wagons.

Surrounded by the carcasses of slain mules and horses, he buried his comrades of the buffalo camp, erecting a rude cross bearing the names of those he had lived and hunted and eaten and slept with during the past three weeks.

All of them, including the golden-bearded Bighorn Ben Kettenring, had been ruthlessly scalped by the departed invaders. The Sioux wipe-out had been as grisly as it had been thorough.

A tingling sensation went through Quent Preston as he finished shaping off the last mound, shortly before noon. He ran splayed fingers through his own unbarbered hair, and realized that only by the grace of Providence had he escaped the gruesome fate of Kettenring and the others.

"I thought that the bottom had dropped out of things when Randle called me last night," went the thought through Preston's head as he replaced his Stetson. "But I reckon the luck's changed for me. Mebbe so from now on things will be looking up for me."

There was nothing to salvage around the scene of death; the Indians had carted off all available guns, knives and other weapons belonging to their victims. The night's rain had blotted out the direction of the Sioux' departure.

Again Preston's eyes rested upon the Wagonwheel paper's headlines which told of the U. P. trail going through his own beloved Tomahawk Pass. Far, far to the southwestward, he could see that pass—a V-shaped depression in the distant Sioux Bonnet range.

His brief career as a buffalo hunter was finished. What lay before him, he did not know. But Preston obeyed his impulse, and headed Alamo toward Tomahawk Pass and the U. P. end-of-track once more.

XXXI

OVERDUE SHOWDOWN

A UNION PACIFIC train snorted through the pines and out into the blazing April sunshine which flooded Tomahawk Pass. A mile beyond, it drew to a halt at a construction-gang camp known as Preston, so called from the name on a blue gypsum tombstone near the bank of Beavertail River.

The field headquarters of the U. P. R. had been pitched near a black bed of embers which, so the track gangs had been told, had been the log cabin belonging to the hapless pioneer whose grave was nearby.

Out of the lone passenger car drawn by the locomotive emerged General G. M. Dodge, chief engineer of the railroad, accompanied by his chief of track layers, General Jack Casement. They made their way immediately to the headquarters tent.

Among the passengers who had ridden out to Tomahawk Pass camp from Wagonwheel City, was a corpulent, muttonchop-whiskered lawyer whose face was familiar along end-of-track. He was Ellis Bayard, the lawyer who had waxed affluent through his right-of-way deals during the building of the line.

Hardly had the paunchy lawyer dismounted from the train than he was met by a black-coated, top-hatted gentleman who was living at the construction camp.

"Boone Delivan, and looking as fit and hearty as ever!" greeted the lawyer, hastening forward to shake the land speculator's hand. "How've things been going out here at end-of-track since you left town, Boone?"

The speculator pointed down the Pass, where gleaming bands of steel stretched off and away toward the Utah border.

"Things have gone fine—with the Union Pacific," clipped the speculator tersely, a cloud of blue cheroot smoke purling from his nostrils. "The reason I sent for you, Bayard, is to know why I haven't been paid for this right-of-way I sold."

Bayard's flabby lips creased in a grin. He fell in step beside Delivan as the latter took his elbow in a firm grip and headed off toward the river bank.

A few yards away from Panhandle Preston's grass-covered grave mound was a small brown tent, which had been Boone Delivan's abode since the time he had sold the Pass right-of-way to the U. P.

Inside the tent, Delivan motioned the corpulent lawyer into a split pole, rawhide-bottomed chair. The speculator seated himself on an army cot and spiked the attorney with a questioning stare.

"I . . . I told you I'd let you know as soon as the money had been paid, Delivan," said the lawyer. "The fact is—"

Delivan shook his head impatiently.

"I'm not interested in facts, nor delays. What I want is the cash money that is coming to me for this right-of-way!"

"But money hasn't come through from the Credit Mobilier yet, Delivan. I—"

The land speculator bent forward, drawing a Colt .45 from an armpit holster. The lawyer paled as Delivan tapped Bayard's knee with the barrel of the weapon.

"With me up here in the Pass protecting my interests, and you down at Wagonwheel City waiting for that money," spoke Delivan evenly, "you might get ideas, Bayard. Like double-crossing me and making off with that money. What's the delay?"

Bayard licked his lips with a dry tongue and gently pushed the speculator's gun muzzle off his knee.

"Only yesterday, I got a letter," panted the lawyer uneasily as he pawed inside his waistcoat pocket. "Here it is. It says the money will be payable around May 10th. By that time, Wagonwheel City will have been disbanded. I wrote the U. P. to mail the money—your money—to my office in Ogden."

Delivan scowled suspiciously.

"You lawyers are so damned scared you won't get your commission," he snarled. "Why couldn't that money be addressed to me—when it was my right-of-way?"

"You forget," purred the lawyer in an oily tone, "that the deal was made through my office, Boone. What chance would you have had to get title to Quent Preston's ranch if I had not . . . er . . . arranged papers and—"

Delivan bounded to his feet, one strong hand clapped over Bayard's flabby mouth.

"Quiet, you blabbering fool!" hissed the speculator. "That kind of talk would put a noose around both our necks. Very well—take the train back to Wagonwheel City this afternoon. But remember, Bayard: I'll be at Ogden on May 10th for that money. You'd better be at your office there—or I'll come gunning for you."

Bayard's breath came in short gasps as he was ushered out of Delivan's tent. The two men stood for a moment alongside Panhandle Preston's grave mound, the significance of which was lost to the Wagonwheel City lawyer, this being his first visit to Tomahawk Pass.

"I have an appointment with General Dodge, to confirm this right-of-way sale," announced Delivan, his glance shifting over to where the U. P. headquarters tent was pitched near the site of Quent Preston's destroyed ranch cabin. "I won't be seeing you when the train leaves—but

I'll be on hand at Ogden to get that money."

Bayard hurried back to the railway tracks to board the train on the siding there, for the return journey to Wagonwheel City. A conductor came through the car with the announcement that the train would leave for the boom town as soon as it had run out to end-of-track to afford some of the U. P. stockholders a glimpse of construction activities.

The pudgy-jowled lawyer began to breathe easier after the snorting locomotive had run three miles up the Pass to the point where red-shirted Irish paddies were toiling under the April sun, laying the rails nearer and nearer Utah.

Bayard had seen much of the railroad's construction, but the bustling activity always fascinated him. He peered out of the railroad car now, watching the dusty activity of the spikers and rail layers.

It was precise work, made into clocklike routine now that the Irish laborers had shoved the tracks across mountain and desert and plain for nearly a thousand miles.

A work engine, shoving a flatcar filled with rails, was at the extreme end of track. Burly paddies would seize the rails and start forward along the roadbed, laying a rail on the new crossties while another crew hastened back to the car for more.

Muscles rippled on naked backs, as spikers

drove their sledges three times to the spike, ten spikes to the rail, four hundred rails to the mile—the famous "anvil chorus in triple time" that was to bridge a nation and link two oceans with steel.

While thus occupied, Ellis Bayard became conscious of a shadow across his car window. He glanced up, to see a sombreroed horseman reined up alongside the roadbed, watching the track layers and spikers at their toil.

Something in the erect carriage of the rider, and the leggy claybank pony on which he rode, made Ellis Bayard screw his brows together in an effort at recalling where he had seen that rider before.

But the sun-tanned face, with its thick growth of dark beard, was no face that Bayard had seen before; and he prided himself on his camera-like memory for faces.

He was in the act of turning his glance away from the rider, when the horseman's glance swiveled to meet his. And in that instant Ellis Bayard's blood turned to water in his veins.

"Quent Preston!"

The whispered name froze on the lawyer's lips, as he saw the bearded horseman stiffen in saddle. Then, before the horrified lawyer could move to slam down the car window, the rider had spurred close alongside the car, his eyes blazing into Bayard's and holding the lawyer fascinated by their stare.

"You're Bayard, ain't you? The lawyer hombre from Wagonwheel—"

Quent Preston's voice was low-pitched and vibrant. It did not ask a question; it stated a fact.

With lithe ease, the cowboy swung out of stirrup and a moment later he had crawled bodily through the window, to drop himself down in the empty seat across from Bayard's. There was no gun in Preston's hand, but the lawyer was held transfixed by the threat of the low-hung Colt .45s thonged to Preston's hips.

"I've waited a plumb long time to meet up with you, Bayard," whispered the cowboy harshly, leaning forward to touch the fat knee that Boone Delivan had tapped with a gun muzzle less than an hour before. "You're going to do some tall talking, Bayard, so don't get spooky and yell for help."

Bayard's mottled face turned the color of raw dough.

"You . . . you can't bully me, Preston—you're a wanted criminal and—"

Bleak fires lighted in the Texan's eyes as he glanced up and down the car. But the stockholders who had taken the train out to end-of-track were too busy watching the construction gangs outside to pay any attention to a conversation between a corpulent lawyer and a buckskin-shirted frontiersman.

"Where's Boone Delivan hiding out, Bayard?"

The lawyer gulped hard. He started to shake his head and deny any knowledge of the speculator's whereabouts, but something in the hard clamp of Preston's mouth behind the unclipped beard told him that the Texan would recognize the lie.

"He's—I just left him—he's at General Dodge's tent—"

Two whistles from the locomotive cut off the lawyer's whisper, and the train car jerked as it started backing down the tracks, slowly gathering speed.

Outside, Preston's claybank pony wheeled and trotted along the tracks alongside the car, following its master.

"We got a date with Boone Delivan, wherever he is, Bayard," whispered Quent Preston, swinging over to sit down by the lawyer.

"You'll . . . be captured . . . you've got a reward on you!" panted Ellis Bayard, his eyes frantic. He broke off at the pressure of Preston's hand on his arm.

"I been a hounded outcast long enough, Bayard," came the Texas cowboy's voice against Bayard's ear. "Maybe I will be arrested. But you and Delivan are going to clear my name—if I get killed making you do it!"

Wilted and limp in the cowboy's grasp, Bayard sat immobile as the train puffed back along the river bank and once more drew to a noisy halt alongside the tents of the construction-gang camp on the site of Preston's ranch.

"Get off—and take me to General Dodge's tent!" ordered Preston, standing up and pulling Bayard to his feet. "If the conductor asks any questions, tell him you're getting off here!"

Sick with fear, the fat lawyer stumbled down the aisle of the car, now filling with men who were intending to ride back through the Pass to Wagonwheel City and points east.

Bayard and his cowboy escort had not walked halfway to General Dodge's headquarters tent when the train got under way once more, cutting off Bayard's only hope of escape.

"This . . . this is foolhardy, Preston!" moaned Bayard, lurching like a drunken man. "Delivan will recognize you. He'll start shooting. There are soldiers inside Dodge's tent. You . . . you wouldn't have a chance!"

Quent Preston loosened his six-guns in their holsters. A grim determination showed in the outthrust lines of his jaw, in the steely glint of his slitted eyes.

Only that morning had he arrived at Tomahawk Pass, and his heart had turned to fire as he had ridden Alamo over the familiar terrain of his ranch, passed his father's grave, and on to the westward for a glance at end-of-track.

"I'm taking that chance, Bayard. If any shooting starts, I'll kill you before they get me.

Remember that—and loosen your tongue when your turn comes to talk. I'm tired of being on the dodge—I'd as soon be dead as live like a slinkin' coyote."

They heard a low mumble of voices as they approached the headquarters tent—Boone Delivan discussing business with the chief engineer of the Union Pacific Railroad, General Dodge.

"String with me, and I'll forget the score I got against you for testifying that I killed that town marshal," whispered Preston. "You know enough to hang Delivan and clear me. Savvy?"

Bayard nodded, his face dewy with sweat as he husked out:

"O. K. But Delivan'll kill you—"

The lawyer staggered forward as Preston gripped his arm and held apart the canvas fly of the tent door. Two more steps, and they were inside the headquarters tent.

General Dodge, an imposing figure behind a table before a spread-out map, looked up with a frown of annoyance at the interruption. Bending over his shoulder was the immaculate figure of the land speculator, Boone Delivan.

"What's this?" demanded General Dodge impatiently, glaring first at Preston and then at the quaking lawyer. "Can't you see we're busy? Get out!"

Boone Delivan's jaw sagged as he peered

harder at Preston's beard-disguised face. One glance at Ellis Bayard's ashen features confirmed Delivan's knowledge that at last he stood face to face with the grim man who had haunted his dreams for weeks.

An ominous smile flickered over Preston's lips as he saw Boone Delivan go white. Even General Dodge caught the menace that charged the atmosphere of the tent.

"Yeah, it's me, Delivan—Quent Preston!" whispered the cowboy. "I'm here for a showdown that's long overdue!"

XXXII

SIX-GUN ACQUITTAL

IN A movement incredibly swift, Boone Delivan kicked back his chair and stabbed a hand to the armpit-holstered .45 he habitually carried.

Before General Dodge or Ellis Bayard could move a muscle, they found themselves in the meshes of a shoot-out between two desperate men.

Quent Preston's six-gun flashed from leather simultaneously with the whipping motion of Delivan's gun arm, as the speculator cleared his Colt muzzle from behind his coat lapel.

In the same motion, Delivan hurled his body behind General Dodge and dropped to a squatting position behind the chief engineer's chair.

Too late, Preston threw down his Colt .45 in a chopping motion at his ducking target. Then he held his fire as he realized that a shot at Delivan would probably mean the death of the U. P.'s chief engineer.

Delivan's gun roared thunderously in the confines of the tent, and flame seared Dodge's coat as the frantic speculator triggered his Colt toward the door of the tent.

But Quent Preston had not been idle during the split heartbeat of time that his adversary was getting behind cover. The Texan hurled himself to the floor of the tent, one shoulder knocking Ellis Bayard out of the line of fire as he did so.

The tent rocked to the deafening crashes of gunfire. Daylight showed through bullet holes that peppered the canvas fly behind Quent Preston as the cowboy charged forward on hands and knees, crawling to get Delivan's range.

With a roar like the old war dog he was, General Dodge shoved the big table to one side and sprang at Preston. Boone Delivan's bullets splintered through the table top, but in the next instant, General Dodge had hurled himself upon the prostrate cowboy and was wrenching at the gun in Preston's hand.

Delivan, rising to a crouch, had one slug left in his Colt. He threw down the gun in a pot shot directed at his erstwhile business partner, Ellis Bayard, and flame and smoke spat from the heavy weapon.

Quent Preston, rearing into a grapple with the wiry old army general, saw a burst of blood gush from the fat lawyer's throat, saw Ellis Bayard collapse like a pricked balloon.

Then, while the cowboy fought desperately to throw off General Dodge, Boone Delivan leaped for the rear of the tent. A knife glittered in his fist and he made a slashing rent down the canvas wall, ducked through the opening and disappeared.

Preston's fist slammed hard up under Dodge's chin, and the fiery-tempered old war general relaxed his husky grip on the cowboy.

Rearing to his feet, Preston dived for the opening in the tent where Boone Delivan had made his escape.

He was in time to see the frock-coated speculator sprinting like an athlete toward the railroad siding that had been built alongside the grave of Panhandle Preston.

A smoking work locomotive was on the siding, its crew busy loading the tender with cordwood from big stacks of pine fuel ricked along the right of way.

With grim purpose, Boone Delivan sped for the locomotive, leaped up into the cab. Preston caught a glimpse of the land buyer's white face as Delivan yanked back the throttle bar.

Desperately punching fired shells from his own Colt, Preston raced toward the track as he saw the locomotive get under way with black smoke belching from its funnel-shaped stack and the drive wheels shedding sparks from steel rails as they whirled under the steam pressure.

A gunshot rang out behind Preston, and a heavy rifle slug zipped inches from Preston's ear to carom off the steel sides of the locomotive beyond.

The cowboy whirled, to see a pair of uniformed soldiers bearing down upon him, one with a naked saber glittering in the sunlight, the other pumping shots at him from a carbine.

Sick with despair, the cowboy from Texas threw up his arms in surrender.

Over his shoulder, he saw the locomotive with Boone Delivan in the cab, crash over the side-track frogs on the main U. P. line and head off toward the east, rapidly gathering speed and leaving a dense fog of blue-black smoke behind.

Out of the headquarters tent came General Dodge, bruised and shaken, but with fiery lights glinting in his eyes.

"Arrest that crazy demon!" shouted the chief engineer, as the two soldiers bore down on Quent Preston. "He's a wanted outlaw—Colonel Sires has a reward outstanding against him!"

Rough hands seized Quent Preston, but there was no despair in the cowboy's eyes as he looked off beyond General Dodge to see Bayard Ellis, the wounded lawyer, staggering out of the tent.

"Bring him inside!" ordered Dodge, his voice shaking. "And what in hell became of Mr. Delivan?"

Preston jerked his head in the direction of the east end of Tomahawk Pass. Already a half mile distant down the tracks, the fugitive locomotive was dwindling in the distance, as Boone Delivan opened the throttle wide.

"Your friend Delivan stole an engine to escape justice, General Dodge," panted Quent Preston, as his soldier guard dragged him up before the chief engineer.

"Delivan—escaping justice?"

"Certainly. Otherwise, why did he attempt to murder Ellis Bayard, yonder—and cut a hole in your tent, and then steal a locomotive to make his getaway in?"

Dodge looked around, to see Ellis Bayard swaying in the doorway of the tent, both hands clutching his blood-spurting neck. For once, Bayard's double chins had served him in good stead; for Delivan's bullet had merely pierced layers of fat, touching no vital artery or muscle.

"This is all very confusing," panted General Dodge, "but one thing is certain—you are in custody, Preston. I have heard of your reputation for being a killer, but I little dreamed you would attempt to commit a murder in my own tent, before my eyes."

Men from surrounding tents were hurrying toward the scene, including the engineer and fireman of the stolen locomotive. General Dodge hurried back inside his tent, ordering one of Preston's captors to stand watch outside to keep curious onlookers away.

"You'd better telegraph to Wagonwheel City for soldiers to capture Delivan, General Dodge!" cried Preston, as he was shoved inside the tent along with Bayard. "Delivan is a killer—and I can prove it, given a few minutes of your time. In the meantime, Delivan's making his getaway—on one of your own Union Pacific engines!"

General Dodge dragged a shaking hand across his eyes, unable to comprehend the tangled events of the past few minutes.

"The engine—yes, yes. I cannot comprehend Mr. Delivan's actions. Orderly! *Orderly!*"

A wide-eyed youth in a blue uniform ducked into the tent and saluted stiffly.

"Orderly, hurry over to the telegraph tent and send a message to the operator at Wagonwheel City to throw open the switch on the siding there. Have an armed guard ready to take Boone Delivan into custody for questioning when he arrives!"

The orderly saluted and ducked from sight.

Then General Dodge stepped over to where Ellis Bayard had sunk down on a camp stool, still clutching bloody fingers to his bullet-pierced double chin.

"You are Mr. Bayard, the attorney?" asked General Dodge. "Can you shed any light on this peculiar situation, Mr. Bayard?"

The lawyer's eyes were wide-rimmed with terror as he looked up at the chief engineer, then over to where Quent Preston stood, a soldier's gun in his back.

"You'd better come clean, Bayard," rasped the cowboy, seeing the lawyer waver. "Boone Delivan tried to murder you, and your life won't

253

be safe if you continue to be on his side. Delivan shot you to keep you from talking."

General Dodge threw up both arms in utter confusion.

"What is this?" groaned the engineer. "Here I am talking routine business with Boone Delivan, and a wanted outlaw comes charging into my tent like a wild bull and a gun fight starts. What's at the bottom of this?"

Ellis Bayard, measuring his own chances of escaping punishment as a crook in league with Boone Delivan, weighed the trend of events and realized that Delivan, and not Quent Preston, was now the fugitive from justice.

Wincing from the pain of his bullet-nicked throat, the lawyer gasped out:

"Preston—is right. Preston's innocent—he's been railroaded into being a criminal. Boone Delivan's the killer you want, general. He's a madman—a fiend."

General Dodge's jaw dropped on an oath of astonishment as information torrented from Ellis Bayard's lips.

Swiftly, desperately, the wounded lawyer poured forth the whole grim story of Boone Delivan's diabolical career—the countless murders he had engineered to further his selfish ambitions, his double-cross of Quent Preston in the matter of Lige Morton's death and the military court-martial which had placed Preston outside the law.

"This Tomahawk Pass—it belongs to Preston!" cried the lawyer, borrowing assurance from the pleased grin on the cowboy's face. "The right of way is his—Delivan forced me at gun's point to forge title papers! I haven't dared to sleep nights or to draw a free breath for months—for fear of being killed by Boone Delivan!"

When the lawyer's babbling recital was finished, Quent Preston stood acquitted of the owl-hoot record against his name.

"That's why I came into the open and declared myself, General Dodge," explained Quent Preston, when Bayard had finished. "I hadn't figured on Delivan beating me to the drop and making a clean getaway so quickly. I knew Bayard could prove my innocence—but I wanted him to talk in front of Delivan and you."

General Dodge sat down on the edge of the upset table and mopped his face with a handkerchief. Then he measured the cowboy with a long, penetrating look, and his grim features softened.

"If what you tell me is the truth, Preston, your innocence can be established by investigating the facts," panted the chief engineer, at last. "And if so, I will arrange your immediate release and the U. P.'s thousand-dollar reward will be canceled."

Excited voices came from outdoors, and a moment later the sentry admitted Lieutenant Colonel Frank Sires, commanding the battalion of United States troops who guarded the railroad against Indian outbreaks.

A glad cry came from Quent Preston as he saw that the army commander was accompanied by Helen Gorine.

XXXIII

TRACKING A KILLER

WITHOUT speaking, the girl disengaged herself from Colonel Sires and flung herself into Preston's arms.

General Dodge turned away with an embarrassed cough as he saw the cowboy take Helen Gorine's lips to his own, his eyes misting with pent-up emotions.

Dodge and the army commander saluted, and the chief engineer swiftly outlined the amazing facts of Preston's innocence of the charges brought against the cowboy at Sires' court-martial.

"I am inclined to believe Preston *is* innocent of the many wrongs attributed to him, General Dodge," was Colonel Sires' statement. "Miss Gorine, here, has acquainted me with several phases of the matter which did not come to light at the court-martial—both as regards Boone Delivan's character, and the facts surrounding the murder of her father and our good friend, Major Gorine. Miss Helen is positive that her father was murdered by or because of Delivan, to keep Major Gorine from testifying to Preston's innocence at the trial."

Ellis Bayard, his courage returned now that he

was aware of the slightness of his neck wound and the fact that he was clearing himself of any complicity with Delivan, spoke up:

"Delivan's opening fire on Mr. Preston, and his subsequent escape on the stolen locomotive, would be considered *prima facie* evidence of Delivan's guilt in a court of law, general."

At that moment they were interrupted by the arrival of an aid, bearing a telegraphic message from a point just outside of Tomahawk Pass. Dodge's face clouded as he read the missive, then looked up at Quent Preston and Colonel Sires.

"Delivan is a clever one," he said. "Listen to this:

"RUNAWAY LOCOMOTIVE WITH NO CREW ABOARD CRASHED HEAD-ON INTO SUPPLY TRAIN WESTBOUND FROM WAGONWHEEL CITY. WRECKING CREW REQUIRED TO CLEAR TRACKS. WIRE INSTRUCTIONS.

"The message is signed by the engineer of the supply train."

Colonel Sires swore fluently.

"That means Delivan jumped off the engine somewhere in the mountains and let it run wild."

Quent Preston, realizing for the first time that the armed soldier behind him had withdrawn the gun from his back, stepped forward eagerly.

258

"Reckon this is where I come in, General Dodge. I got a fast horse outside, and I can read sign as good as an Injun. If Boone Delivan is runnin' loose in Tomahawk Pass, I can find out where he jumped the engine and I can track him down."

Dodge smiled at the eagerness in the cowboy's voice, and turned to Sires, who nodded.

"Very well, Preston. You are free to go. My only stipulation is that you bring Delivan in alive, if possible. Kill him only if forced to do so in self-defense."

A pulse throbbed in the Texan's neck as he looked down into Helen Gorine's troubled eyes. As yet, the lovers had not had a chance to speak of the thousand things that clamored in their hearts for expression.

"Don't worry about me, Helen. I'll be back, pronto—draggin' Boone Delivan by the heels."

"But he might ambush you, Quent—there's so much at stake—"

Gently, Preston disengaged himself from the girl's clinging arms. He loosened the six-guns in his holsters with grim resolution.

"I got a job to do, Helen. I've always been at a disadvantage, fightin' Delivan. He's got education and polish. But they won't do him no good if he's afoot out here in the wilds. This is my country, not his."

With a final pressure of his hand and a word of

thanks to the military men about him, Quent Preston ducked out of the tent.

A few yards away, Alamo awaited him, having followed him back to the camp. Once in saddle, Preston waved his sombrero in farewell to Helen and the men grouped about her at the door of General Dodge's tent, and spurred off down the U. P. tracks toward the mouth of Tomahawk Pass.

Riding the right of way, he followed the curving tracks through the forests where he had once seen Major Gorine running the survey that was to make the martyred engineer famous in the annals of the Union Pacific.

Westering sunlight was at his back when he emerged from Tomahawk Pass, his eyes studying every inch of the soft shale roadbed which flanked the tracks.

Two miles out of the pass, he caught sight of the wrecked supply train to the eastward. Somewhere between the spot where he now rode and the train wreck, Boone Delivan had quit his runaway locomotive.

Not a hundred yards farther on, the cowboy's alert eyes caught sight of deep gouges in the roadbed, where a pair of boots had dug into the soft earth.

Plainly visible in the soil were the marks of hand prints, where Boone Delivan had sprawled after his leap from the locomotive he had commandeered.

Delivan's tracks led away from the right of way and into the sage-dotted flats, a trail easy to follow, even for a tenderfoot.

The surrounding terrain offered no refuge for an ambusher. Therefore, the cowboy spurred Alamo into a trot, following the path taken by the escaping speculator.

He had traveled less than half a mile on Delivan's trail when sundown overtook him, followed swiftly by nightfall.

"Nothing I can do but camp here and pick up the tracks with daylight," decided Preston, dismounting. "It's a cinch Delivan won't get far, on foot."

He made a dry camp a quarter of a mile distant from the outlaw's trail, on the summit of a small knoll. He could take no chances on Delivan doubling back and gunning him as he slept.

The night passed uneventfully, and the first ruddy streaks of daylight found Preston in the saddle and riding back to where Delivan's trail showed plainly in the sagebrush.

Following it, Preston saw that Delivan had turned due east, in the direction of Wagonwheel City. The country remained open, and no glimpse of the fugitive could the sharp-eyed cowboy discern ahead of him.

During the night, wrecking crews had cleared the track where Delivan's engine had smashed into the supply train, and the train had been hauled by a reserve engine to end-of-track.

Two hours later, Preston caught sight of another train puffing its way toward Wagonwheel City, from Tomahawk Pass. Delivan's tracks were paralleling the railroad, heading without a stop, toward the construction camp.

"The loco fool must be getting back to town, walking all night!" grunted Preston, a tinge of admiration in his voice—admiration for the fierce will and iron stamina of the speculator.

A night wind had scoured the flats, wiping out Delivan's trail and forcing Preston to ride in wide circles before picking it up at occasional points.

Delivan's shoes were dragging the dirt, but his trail was still pointing toward Wagonwheel City. It seemed incredible that the speculator could have covered the forty-odd miles during the night, but as Preston rode in sight of the boom camp at Wagonwheel Springs he still had seen no trace of the fugitive.

As he approached the boom town, Preston was surprised to see scores of creaking wagons plodding westward along the ruts flanking the U. P. R. The wagons were laden with lumber, folded tents, and the knocked-down sections of saloons and dance halls.

As Preston passed some of the wagons, he could even read painted signs on some of the boards carried by the wagons, signs which he and Panhandle had read the first minute they had stumbled across the railroad town: End-of-Track Hotel; Red Tent Saloon; Shamrock Livery Stables.

"Looks like it's *adios* to Wagonwheel City," grunted Preston, as he neared the outskirts of the town. "And I can't say as I'm sorry."

It was true. Wagonwheel City, like the dozens of flourishing construction towns before it, was dying. Already multitudes of individual tents had been taken down and carted on railroad cars and freight wagons westward.

As he rode up the main street toward the willow-rimmed waterhole, he saw that the big saloons and dance halls had been taken down. There was feverish activity there yet, but not the maudlin type of action Preston had seen on previous visits to the mushroom city.

The army barracks were gone; the great End-of-Track Hotel was a thing of the past. Soon all that would be left of Wagonwheel City would be mounds of rubbish, tin cans, littered boards, and the grim cemetery with its unmarked graves up on the stump-dotted hillside.

The eternal rocks and the sage flats would be there for all time to come, and Wagonwheel Springs; but the scars made by man would be covered by winter snows, and gradually erased by nature's blowing sand and sprouting grass.

Somehow, the sight brought solace to Quent Preston, as he passed Wagonwheel Springs and threaded his horse through the milling wagon teams and horse herds and the shouting, restless folk who had populated Wagonwheel City in its wicked heyday.

A voice hailed Preston excitedly by name, as the cowboy passed the vacant lot that had been occupied by the Union Pacific office. He reined over, to see Ellis Bayard standing beside the steps of his tiny canvas-roofed Land Office.

Bayard had come back to Wagonwheel City on the eastbound train Preston had seen earlier that morning. The lawyer's neck was girdled with bandages. Bayard was talking excitedly with a lanky individual dressed in the woolen Mackinaw and warped boots of a mule-skinner.

"Preston, I've got word of Delivan's whereabouts here!" shouted the lawyer excitedly, as the cowboy swung from saddle before them. "Delivan's sent me a message! Look!"

The Texan started. Delivan had indeed accomplished the impossible, if he had beaten Preston to town. Only sheer desperation could have driven the speculator across the badlands through the night, on foot and without pausing for rest.

Ellis Bayard thrust a sheet of notebook paper into Quent's grasp. Squinting his eyes against the glare of Wyoming sunlight on the white paper, the cowboy read a hastily-scribbled message:

BAYARD: I'm laying low until May 10th. You know where to be on that date. If you aren't there with the money, you won't live long enough to doublecross anybody again.
                                                BOONE DELIVAN.

Preston looked up, scanning the flabby-jowled lawyer intently, not knowing if this was a ruse or not.

"Did Delivan give you this, Bayard?"

The lawyer jerked his head toward the crudely-dressed mule-skinner beside him.

"No. Delivan ran across this man's camp on Bitterroot Ridge late last night. He paid this man fifty dollars for a horse, twenty dollars for a saddle, and ten dollars to look me up here in Wagonwheel and deliver this message."

Cold dread gripped Preston's heart as he absorbed this crushing knowledge. Delivan, caught at a hopeless disadvantage out in the wilds, had outwitted the cowboy by bribing a plainsman to sell him a horse.

"What time of night did Delivan buy your bronc, feller?" demanded Preston, turning to the mule-skinner.

"I'd already turned in. Reckon, judgin' from where the stars was, it was midnight."

"What did Delivan do after you'd sold him a horse?"

"Lit a shuck toward the railroad track, after

265

he'd writ that note an' told me that this lawyer feller would pay me another twenty bucks fer deliverin' it. I walked to town an' found Ellis Bayard an' give him this feller's note."

Preston glanced down at the paper, rereading Delivan's threat to violence.

"You savvy this message, Bayard?" he asked.

The muttonchopped lawyer nodded excitedly, his eyes mirroring the fear in Bayard's heart.

"Yes. The money for the Tomahawk Pass right of way is due May tenth. Boone Delivan was to meet me at my office in Ogden, Utah, and get the money."

Preston was silent a long while, pondering. He realized the uselessness of trying to track Boone Delivan; the speculator's head start was too much, and the wind had doubtlessly erased his tracks. Nor was there any way of guessing where Delivan would go to hole up until May tenth.

"Bayard, your life won't be worth a white chip so long as Delivan is on the loose. You realize that?"

"Yes." Bayard gulped. "Delivan's after me."

"Then you have that right-of-way money ready for him in Ogden on May tenth, Bayard. That's only two weeks off. I'll see to it that Boone Delivan doesn't collect it. The only thing he'll collect will be a hangman's knot—or a bullet."

266

XXXIV

DELIVAN PLAYS HIS ACE

EXCITEMENT reigned throughout Utah as May ninth dawned. The event which America, and the entire world, had awaited for so many years was due to materialize on the morrow—the joining of the Union Pacific rails with those of the Central Pacific, built eastward from the California gold country.

Promontory Point, a bleak, wind-swept desert stretching out into the blue platter that was Great Salt Lake, had been chosen by destiny as the point where rails would meet and America would be linked by steel, a continent conquered by man's might.

Ogden was jammed to overflowing with cowboys and miners, prospectors and Indian fighters, covered-wagon drivers. The riffraff who had peopled the end-of-track towns for over a thousand miles out from Omaha were there, too, adding a tawdry splash to the riot of color—gamblers and professional gunmen, painted hussies from the dance halls, saloonmen and freighters, barflies and blacksmiths.

Sombreroed outlaws rubbed shoulders with silk-hatted businessmen out from the East to see the momentous "wedding of the rails;" in the air was a din of Chinese voices from the vast army of coolies who had built the Central Pacific tracks across the Western desert malpais; while mingled with the newcomers were the dark-bearded, solemn-faced Mormons, case-hardened men who had originally won this sun-parched land for their home, setting up a city beside the great inland sea whose waters were tinctured with bitter chemicals.

Quent Preston, once more dressed in the gray Stetson, blue shirt and brass-studded bat-wing chaps of the Texas plains, rode his claybank pony through the jammed streets, enjoying the bustle and excitement attending the completion of the U. P. R.

Heavy six-guns were at his thighs, sagging the cartridge-studded gun belts which looped his flanks; a new .30-.30 Winchester carbine reposed in the boot under Alamo's saddle. The weapons seemed in keeping with the brittle gleam of the cowboy's eyes, as they swept the teeming throngs of humanity.

He threaded his horse through the polished buggies and heavy-wheeled freight wagons and dust-grimed prairie schooners which jammed Ogden's principal street, and found space for his cow-pony at a crowded hitch rack in front of a saloon.

The second story of the saloon was given over to offices, and painted on the glass window of one of the rooms was a sign which had been his goal:

ELLIS BAYARD, LAWYER
LAND TITLES—R. R. STOCK

Across the street, in the Brigham Young Hotel, Preston knew that Helen Gorine would be awaiting his arrival in the Utah town. The daughter of the U. P.'s courageous survey chief had been the first white woman to make the train journey across the Wyoming-Utah boundary, over the new railroad through Tomahawk Pass.

Hitching his gun belts into a more comfortable position, Preston made his way into the Brigham Young. He had hardly entered the lobby before a glad cry rang out through the hubbub and he was holding out his arms to Helen Gorine, now clad in a cool white frock and looking daintily feminine, with her chestnut hair held in place by a ribbon of orange silk.

"Some different from the girl in pants who saved my life from a panther in Tomahawk Pass, eh, Helen?" laughed the cowboy, glancing behind Helen to see General Dodge and Ellis Bayard, the land-office attorney. "But you'll always look like a gold nugget to me, I reckon."

General Dodge extended a hand in greeting to the cowboy.

"You'll be glad to know, Mr. Preston, that the Tomahawk Pass right of way has been transferred back to you," smiled the Union Pacific chief. "Mr. Bayard tells me that during the past week he has received a telegram from Washington to the effect that your homestead rights have been restored."

A vast contentment filled Preston's heart as he saw the look on Ellis Bayard's beaming face, and in that moment the Texan forgave the corpulent lawyer for all his illegal work as Boone Delivan's partner.

"That means the Lone Star Ranch is yours again, Preston," chuckled the lawyer. "If you'll come up to my office, we'll fix up the final details. And in view of circumstances, I won't be charging you any fee."

General Dodge moved away, summoned by important-looking personages from the big cities in the East who were making the hotel their headquarters.

"Helen, suppose you excuse me and Mr. Bayard, will you?" said the cowboy, turning to the girl at his side. "I won't be seeing you until the golden spike ceremonies out at Promontory Point tomorrow. Me and Bayard got a business deal on that'll occupy all of my attention."

The girl's eyes clouded with disappointment, but she nodded. As yet, Bayard or Preston had not informed her of the trap they were laying for Boone Delivan.

"All right, Quent. But don't fail to be on the U. P. passenger train tomorrow. This—this means an awful lot to me, this wedding of the rails. It's the day my father prayed he would be able to see—

and I want you to take his place by my side when we see the last spike driven."

After the girl had lost herself in the crowded lobby, making her way back toward her hotel room, Preston and Bayard headed for the street.

"It'll be a good idea if I hide myself in your office today, Bayard," said the cowboy. "We can't take any chances of Boone Delivan seeing me, and flying the coop."

Perspiration oozed from Bayard's pores, and a shiver of apprehension went through the fat lawyer as he contemplated his part in springing the trap that would put the crooked speculator in the grip of justice.

"It's in the bag, Preston," reassured the lawyer. "Delivan won't miss trying to collect the forty thousand dollars for that right of way through the pass. He's sure to show up."

Preston grinned with suppressed excitement.

"And I'll be waiting for the skunk," muttered the Texan.

At that moment, Helen Gorine was climbing the stairway to the upper floor of the frontier hotel. She unlocked the door to the room she had engaged, and entered.

Even as she shut the door behind her, Helen caught sight of the curtained door of her clothes closet stirring—yet no wind was stirring the curtains of the open window overlooking the roofs of adjoining Ogden buildings.

A swift foreboding filled the girl. Before she could move in the direction of the dresser where she had left a Colt six-gun, the closet curtains parted.

There, crouching not five feet away, stood Boone Delivan.

A leveled .45 was in the speculator's hand, the bore aimed at Helen's heart. The outlaw's face, burned a deep tan by his week of hiding out in the desert, was twisted into a mask of hate as he stalked forward.

"Not a sound, Helen!" warned Delivan, his teeth glinting behind slitted lips. "I won't kill you if you obey orders."

The girl cringed in horror as Delivan shot out an arm and clamped viselike fingers about her elbow. Whiskey was thick on the land-buyer's breath as he drew her to him.

"I spotted Quent Preston in town just now," whispered the crooked speculator venomously. "And that means some doublecross is in the wind. So I intend to have an ace in the hole—and you're that card!"

Helen Gorine recovered herself, wrenched sharply at Delivan's clamping fingers.

"You're a coward, Delivan. You wouldn't dare harm me—"

Fiendish lights glittered in Delivan's slotted eyes.

"No? You still think me the polished gentleman,

eh? I wasn't above stabbing your father in his sleep, was I? Does that sound as if I wouldn't dare harm you—"

Delivan's brutal confession of slaying Major John Gorine in Wagonwheel City, the night before Preston's court-martial, had its intended effect on the steel-nerved girl.

She wilted in his crushing grasp, momentarily overcome by the shocking truth of her own suspicions—

Before she could recover from the mental shock of Delivan's words, the outlaw holstered his gun and whipped a silken scarf from the pocket of his frock coat.

Swiftly, Delivan wedged the scarf between Helen's jaws and knotted it tightly behind her neck, gagging her so that no outcry was possible.

Then, whipping a coil of light rope from his pocket, Delivan knotted her wrists tightly behind her back.

Hurling her roughly to the floor, Delivan bound the girl's ankles in similar fashion. Then he made his way to the closet and dragged out Helen's big trunk, filled with personal belongings of herself and her murdered father.

Swiftly emptying the trunk of its contents, Delivan lifted the dazed girl and wedged her inside. Clamping down and locking the lid clasps, Delivan then took a heavy bowie knife from a concealed sheath at his belt and with hard stabbing motions, made a pair of ventilating holes in the trunk's cowhide lid.

That done, the spectator calmly wiped his face and hands with a breast pocket handkerchief. He paused a moment to shove the contents of the trunk under the bed, and then made his way to the window overlooking a back alley of the hotel.

Below, his henchman Jeb Franklin waited with an empty-saddled horse. A ladder extended from Helen's window to the ground, the ladder by which Delivan had gained entry to the girl's room a scant twenty minutes before.

There was no one to see the frock-coated outlaw as he hurried down the ladder, lifted it aside and thrust it under the foundation timbers of the hotel floor. Then he put foot to stirrup and swung aboard the horse, accepting the reins which Franklin passed him.

"Everything ready, boss?" questioned the gunhawk.

Delivan nodded.

"She's in the trunk. She won't smother, and she's gagged so she can't make an outcry. When night comes, lower her out the window, trunk and all. Make sure the trunk is aboard the night train running over to Promontory Point. Take her from there by horseback out to our hideaway. I will meet you there around midnight."

"I get you, boss."

"And don't fail, Franklin. You don't get paid for this one last job for me—if I don't collect that Tomahawk Pass money from Bayard tomorrow. And us having Helen Gorine will make sure we get that money, if trouble comes!"

XXXV

KIDNAPER'S PAYOFF

QUENT PRESTON crouched in a stuffy office adjoining that of Ellis Bayard, the attorney. He was peering through a keyhole into Bayard's office, keeping an eye on the bald-headed lawyer as the latter pretended to be concentrating on the papers at his desk.

The Texas cowboy had spent the past night keeping sleepless vigil beside Ellis Bayard's office, which was to be Boone Delivan's rendezvous with his erstwhile partner in outlawry.

Morning light now streamed in through the open window behind Bayard. On the desk at the lawyer's elbow was a thick envelope, filled with greenbacks—a fortune in cash, representing the staggering sum which the U. P. R. had paid for the right-of-way through the Lone Star ranch in Tomahawk Pass.

Preston's heart slammed with suspense. He had inspected his six-guns a dozen times since sunup that morning. Yet Boone Delivan had not appeared, and it was past nine o'clock.

And then, as a clock somewhere was booming the quarter hour, a knock came on Ellis Bayard's door. Preston saw the lawyer turn a shade whiter, as he called out in a trembling voice for the knocker to come in.

Shifting his position at the keyhole, Preston saw the door open and Boone Delivan entered. A bulge at the speculator's armpit told of the Colt six-gun which nestled there. Delivan's handsome face was taut and strained, but a triumphant gleam was in the land-buyer's eyes as he crossed the floor and stood in front of Bayard.

"So, my good friend Bayard—you did not turn yellow and try to run out on me? You have the money?"

Bayard thrust the fat envelope filled with money across the table. His voice was a creaky squawk as he answered the leering speculator:

"There it is—less my commission. Take it and get out, Delivan. This is our last business deal— and I'm lucky I didn't get my neck stretched, teaming up with you!"

The cowboy hidden in the next room saw Delivan's eyes flash with greed as he seized the envelope, tore it open and riffled swiftly through the bundle of currency.

"You see, I don't trust you—to the end!" whispered Boone Delivan, thrusting the money into an inner pocket. "And now, I have one last present for you—as a token of my deep regard for you, my fat pig friend—"

Quent Preston was not prepared for what happened next. He saw Delivan's hand emerge from his coat, after putting the money for the Tomahawk Pass right of way into his pocket.

But as Delivan's hand came into the open, it clutched a razor-edged bowie knife, the blade of which dazzled Preston's eyes in the bright sunlight.

In a motion that caught Bayard in the act of leaning forward to accept Delivan's parting gift, the speculator thrust the knife blade foremost across the table.

There was a grisly sound, like a knife sinking into a slab of butter. When Delivan released the haft, six inches of keen-whetted steel were embedded in the lawyer's heart.

Even as Ellis Bayard sagged in his chair in death, Boone Delivan spun about and took a step forward toward the door.

Then the killer halted stock-still, as the door in the side wall swung open to reveal Quent Preston on the threshold, a Colt .45 in his right hand, thumb earing the knurled hammer to full cock.

"You damned—" panted the cowboy, as he stalked forward, eyes blazing with hatred. "You put one over on me, murdering Bayard—"

The floor shook as the murdered lawyer's corpse toppled from the swivel chair to sprawl behind the desk. But neither man heard it, as they faced each other across the death-hushed office.

Boone Delivan's flushed face had gone oyster-gray, as he stared at death down the bore of

Preston's gun. He saw the cowboy's knuckle whiten under pressure at the Colt's trigger.

Then, with a supreme effort, Delivan got control of himself and was once more the smiling, cold-eyed gentleman who had cowed gunmen more than once in his tempestuous past.

"If you shoot me, Preston, you are signing Helen Gorine's death warrant."

Preston's jaw dropped. Something in the grim assurance of Delivan's voice told the cowboy that this was no desperate bluff on the speculator's part. Delivan held a surprise card in the hole.

"At this minute," went on Delivan, his eyes still fixed to the muzzle of the six-gun aimed at his midriff, "Helen Gorine is my prisoner. One of my men is guarding her, with orders to put a bullet in her head if I am not back by noon."

The gun in Preston's hand quivered ever so slightly. The seething rage in the cowboy's heart turned to cold despair, leaving him gaunt and spent.

"You're lying, Delivan. You're bluffing. Trying to keep me from gunning you to hell."

Delivan shrugged, started to reach in his pocket, then halted as he saw Preston whip up his gun, crouching defensively.

"I'm not reaching for a gun, Preston. I have proof in my pocket that Helen is in my keeping."

Preston, seeing that Delivan's coat pocket held no telltale bulge of knife or derringer, relaxed.

"Hand it over."

Delivan reached in his pocket and produced a band of orange-colored silk ribbon. He handed it to Preston, who went white as he recognized it as the ribbon, bearing Helen Gorine's monogram, which she had worn on her head the afternoon before.

"I had a hunch Ellis Bayard might be scheming some sort of doublecross, trying to trap me," taunted the speculator. "That was why—as always—I came prepared for any eventuality. Did you think I was such a stupid fool as to trust Bayard—when I tried to kill him back in Tomahawk Pass and failed?"

Preston's head spun as he clenched the ribbon in his fist, remembering how Helen Gorine had pressed that ribbon against his breast in the hotel lobby only a few hours before.

"I'll kill you for this, Delivan—where before I was planning to turn you over to the law." Preston's voice was dead.

"And make no effort to save Helen's life?"

The Texan's hand went limp, dropping Helen Gorine's ribbon to the floor. He knelt to recover it, and in that instant Boone Delivan leaped like a berserk animal upon the crouching man.

Spang! The heavy Colt in Preston's hand exploded deafeningly as Preston fired instinctively, not intending to do so.

Delivan's leap was checked in mid-air. A

ghastly look crossed the speculator's face, and his eyes glazed over like unpolished marbles in their sockets.

Then, with a shudder, Boone Delivan collapsed at Preston's feet and lay motionless.

"What have I done? I've killed him without knowing where Helen is being held prisoner—"

In an agony of despair, Preston turned over Delivan's body with the toe of his boot. The speculator's black frock coat fell open, exposing Preston's bullet hole in his waistcoat.

At the same instant, the cowboy saw a pulse throbbing on Delivan's neck, proving that the point-blank shot had not killed him instantly.

Holstering his fuming Colt, Preston stooped, felt of the thick bulge in the waistcoat pocket immediately beneath the bullet hole in the fabric.

A moment later he was pulling out the thick sheaf of United States currency which Boone Delivan had thrust into the pocket. Most of the bills were perforated by the tunneling .45 slug. But inside the thick sheaf of greenbacks was the misshapen lump of lead which was Preston's bullet.

A rush of thanksgiving coursed through the cowboy's being as he realized that the bullet, hitting Delivan at an oblique angle, had spent its force in the thick wad of paper. The money for Preston's Tomahawk Pass homestead right of way had been a shield to keep the slug from penetrating Delivan's heart!

Pocketing the money with its embedded slug, Preston stooped and lifted Boone Delivan, carrying him over to Bayard's desk. The lawyer kept a pitcher of water filled with floating chunks of ice, and now Preston dumped the contents of the pitcher over Delivan's unconscious head and neck.

Even as the knocked-out speculator began blinking himself back to his senses, Preston frisked him swiftly, removing a heavy Frontier Model Colt from Preston's armpit holster and a pair of deadly single-shot derringers from the sleeves of the gambler's coat which the speculator wore.

As Delivan came back to consciousness, Preston reamed the barrel of his Colt into the land buyer's midriff and, seizing him by the front of the collar, jerked him into a sitting position.

"You're taking me to Helen Gorine, Delivan— or I'll kill you before we leave this room!"

Delivan shook his head to clear it. He knew that the cowboy held him at his mercy; knew that Quent Preston had been goaded to the limit of his endurance.

For the first time in his criminal career, Delivan felt the icy fingers of terror clutching him. He recoiled from the gun jammed against his body, and nervous sweat dripped from his pores as he struggled to speak.

"O.K. . . . Preston. You win. All I ask . . . is a chance to make my getaway . . . after I turn . . . Helen over to you!"

Preston swallowed his rage at Delivan's having the gall to demand a compromise, here in the very shadow of eternity. But to the Texan, the life of Helen Gorine meant vastly more than the pleasure of satisfying his revenge against the snake who was now crawling before him in surrender.

"All right, Delivan. I'll bargain with you. I'll turn you loose—the minute I have Helen safe beside me. Where is she?"

Delivan passed a shaking hand over his chest, where flesh was bruised and throbbing from the terrific impact of the bullet which had so miraculously been turned aside.

"One of my men—Jeb Franklin—keeping her prisoner in a sheepherder's shack—north of Promontory Point. Took her there—on last night's train—then to the sheepherder's shack by pack horse."

Preston groaned. Promontory Point, where the rail-joining rites were to be held that afternoon, was a full thirty miles away. He had no way of knowing how much farther Helen Gorine's kidnap shack would be from U. P. tracks. And at noon, Helen was to be put to death by Jeb Franklin.

"I'll get General Dodge to rush us out to the Point on a special car, Delivan. And remember— I'm desperate. If I find Helen dead—or if you're trying a doublecross—I'll shoot you down like a sidewinder."

XXXVI

DEATH IN THE DESERT

HELEN GORINE struggled in her bonds, staring wildly through disheveled strands of hair about the stuffy confines of the rock cabin in which she had been kept prisoner since midnight. Jeb Franklin, the coarse-visaged gunhawk who had transported her from the U. P. tracks at Promontory Point by means of a pack horse, had removed her from the trunk in which she had been taken on the railroad train the night before, and had lashed her securely to a broken-down chair in the middle of the room.

"It's five minutes to twelve," growled Franklin, consulting a gold watch which he had filched from the corpse of a gun-fight victim in a saloon back in Wagonwheel City months before. "The chief told me to put a slug in your noggin an' make my own getaway, if he wasn't back here by noon."

The girl swallowed back panic which filled her being. She had been tied too tightly to the chair to have any chance at escape. And she knew the hairy ruffian would make good his orders.

Helen Gorine cried out in alarm as she saw Franklin pocket his watch and turn to face her, murder blazing in his red-rimmed orbs. Slowly,

285

the killer slipped a long-barreled Colt from its holster at his thigh.

"Time's up," panted Franklin hoarsely. "I ain't hankerin' to kill a woman, miss, but orders is orders, an' I got my own hide to think about!"

The girl froze in her bonds as she saw Franklin level the gun at her head. Then, through the window behind him, she caught sight of two riders appearing around a heavy rock outcrop down the hillside below the sheepherder's shack.

"Wait—wait! There's Delivan—"

Franklin whirled about, jumped to the window. Then he stiffened as he saw that Boone Delivan was not alone.

Riding alongside the frock-coated speculator's stirrup was a lanky rider on a claybank pony, his Stetson shoved back from a dust-grimed face, a gun flashing in the sunlight from the rider's hand.

"Delivan's been took prisoner!"

Helen Gorine gasped in mingled joy and alarm as she, too, recognized the cowpuncher who was spurring up the slope alongside Boone Delivan. Even at this distance, she recognized that lanky horseman as Quent Preston, not some other henchman of Delivan's.

With a foul oath, Jeb Franklin leaped to the wall where he had leaned a Winchester rifle.

Thrusting the barrel over the weather-beaten window sill, Franklin notched the sights on Quent Preston's chest.

Then, before he could pull trigger, Boone Delivan's yell came up the hillside to check him:

"Franklin! Franklin! Don't do any shooting—I'm in a tight spot!"

At the same moment, Helen Gorine saw Quent Preston spur over behind Delivan's horse, so as to put the speculator between him and the scowling killer inside the shack.

"Come outside, Franklin!" yelled Boone Delivan, his voice harsh and cracked. "If you don't, I'll be blasted off this horse sure as hell!"

Franklin withdrew his rifle, cursing under his breath. With a quick glance at the helpless girl tied to the chair, the killer went to the door and stepped out into the hot sunshine.

Boone Delivan drew rein not fifty feet from the cabin, and Helen Gorine got a clear view of Quent Preston as the Texas cowboy spurred Alamo close in behind Delivan, wary of any ambush fire from the shack.

"You all right, Helen?" came the Texan's anxious yell.

Tears flooding her eyes in the ecstasy of her relief, the imprisoned girl shouted back:

"Yes, yes! But be careful, Quent. Very—"

Wary as a stalking cougar, Preston swung out of saddle. Both six-guns were in his hands, as he halted alongside Delivan's horse and clipped through the corner of his mouth:

"Tell your sidewinder pard to drop that rifle and come out here with his hands up, Delivan!"

His words carried to Jeb Franklin, who was torn between a desire to leap back into the shelter of the rockwalled cabin, and the necessity of obeying Delivan's orders.

Accordingly, Franklin tossed aside his .30-.30 and walked down the slope toward them, his hands, above the level of his Stetson brim.

"All right, Delivan," snarled Preston. "I'm keeping my side of the bargain. Soon as I make sure Helen's safe, I'm letting you and your paid killer vamose. But make sure you keep travelin'—because if our trails ever cross again, I start foggin' my guns!"

Franklin halted a few feet away from them, and a swift message flashed from his eyes to Delivan's. The speculator, without weapons, was not tied up, nor had he been since they had boarded their horses at Promontory Point for the ten-mile ride into the northern desert.

"Step over here, Franklin!" ordered Quent Preston, as the hair-jowled ruffian hesitated. "I'm taking your guns. Then I'm herding you and Delivan inside that shack, to untie Helen. Once I'm sure she's *bueno,* I'll let you two skunks loose. But not till then!"

Franklin halted at arm's length from Preston. The cowboy holstered his left-hand gun, and reached forward to unbuckle Franklin's cartridge belts.

288

In that instant, Boone Delivan swung out of saddle and dropped, both hands outstretched, to block an upward movement of Quent Preston's gun arm.

With a fiendish roar, Jeb Franklin stabbed both hands to his own guns, then buckled in the middle as Preston's gun bucked and spat flame, the bullet slamming Franklin in the pit of the stomach.

Before he could leap aside, Boone Delivan's crushing weight knocked Preston to the ground. Strangling fingers closed about Preston's throat, choking the breath from his lungs as Delivan pinned the cowboy's gun wrist into the dirt.

XXXVII

THE GOLDEN SPIKE

PRESTON released his grip on the Colt as he felt his senses fading. Desperately, he rolled over on his back and clawed both hands at the throttling fingers which Boone Delivan had clamped about his windpipe.

The sheer ferocity of his defense tore the choking fist from his neck. Delivan drove skin-crushing blows with his other fist into Preston's jaw and eyes and mouth, the rocky earth, making it impossible for the cowboy to roll his head from under the damaging punches.

With frantic strength, Preston clamped one hand about the wrist of Delivan's pommeling arm, halted the terrific onslaught of blows.

Then Delivan jumped to his feet and backed away, launching an agonizing kick to Preston's short ribs that broke bone and drove the breath from his lungs.

Dazed and bleeding, Preston rolled to one side and reared to his feet as he saw Delivan stooping to reach for the six-gun which Preston had dropped underfoot.

Summoning his flagging senses, Preston launched himself at the stooping outlaw, rocked Delivan's head on his shoulders with a smoking haymaker.

Off balance, Delivan's back struck hard against the withers of the horse standing behind him. Rebounding like a rubber ball, the speculator smashed into the groggy cowboy before Preston could claw out the second six-gun in the holster at his side.

Toe to toe the two men stood, exchanging uppercuts and lightning jabs. Evenly matched as to weight and reach, the two were met in primitive combat, each questing for the other's life.

Preston was knocked spinning as a terrific blow landed on his jaw, stunning him. Screaming like a maniac, Boone Delivan charged in with flailing boots and outstretched hands to press his advantage and deliver the knockout blow that would enable him to blow out Preston's brains when he could get a gun in hand.

Through clouding dust, Preston saw the outlaw's charge, cranked up his knees and lashed out with both high-heeled boots to catch Delivan squarely in the chest.

As the outlaw staggered backward under the countermove, Preston gained a precious second of time in which to regain his feet.

Wiping sweat and blood from his eyes, the cowboy saw Boone Delivan stumble to his knees, then saw sunlight glitter blindingly as the speculator snatched up Preston's fallen Colt.

With automatic motion of his left arm, the

cowboy seized the rubber stock of his own holstered .45. There was no time to draw and cock the weapon; already, Delivan's gun was thundering.

Preston squeezed trigger, felt the tug of the holster against his shell belt as the bullet ripped through the end of the scabbard.

He felt a bullet smash through the muscles of his right thigh, as Delivan's second shot struck home. He triggered his holstered gun again, firing blindly at the berserk devil before him.

Then Boone Delivan's gun ceased bucking and roaring. The speculator tried to pull himself to his feet, but his knees had unhinged and he pitched, face forward, on the dirt.

Suddenly sick with shock and relief, Preston turned away from the dead outlaw and staggered toward the sheepherder's cabin, and Helen.

Two hours later, Quent Preston and Helen Gorine arrived back at Promontory Point, to see the thrilling spectacle of a Union Pacific locomotive puffing impatiently, a few yards to the west of a Central Pacific engine.

Flags flew everywhere; a brass band from California had just finished the national anthem; and as the trail-dusty man and girl dismounted from their horses at the outskirts of the throng, an orator who was one of the greatest men of his age, was shouting to the assembled multitude:

"In precisely one more minute, ladies and gentlemen, the single word *'Done!'* will be flashed by telegraph to waiting people throughout America."

A cry rang out from the dignitaries grouped between the waiting locomotives on the track, and the voice of General Dodge interrupted the orator:

"One moment, if you will! We must add to the list of the great men and humble, who have built this road across a continent, we must pay honor to one who cannot be with us—Major John Gorine, whose engineering genius made it possible for the Union Pacific to reach this spot—I see his daughter among us, even now—"

Quent Preston was at Helen Gorine's side as they were escorted through the cheering throngs, to a point of honor alongside the tracks.

Arm and arm, they watched while a spike of shimmering solid gold was placed in position alongside the rail, and honored men of the day were allowed one stroke of the sledge each.

And, as the golden spike was hammered home to bridge a nation, one corner of the soft yellow metal gouged against the iron rail to form a curled shaving of pure California gold.

It was General Dodge who stooped to pick up the sliver of gold and press it into Quent Preston's hand.

Helen Gorine, looking up into the eyes of the

Texas cowboy at her side, saw him stoop to whisper against her ear:

"This piece of golden spike will make a fine wedding ring, Helen, for you to wear when you're the mistress of our Lone Star ranch."

They held each other in close embrace as the locomotive whistles blasted the day and men celebrated a wedding already achieved.

Her soft answer was lost in the roar of acclaim which went up as the two Iron Horses touched noses at the end of the trail.

Center Point Publishing
600 Brooks Road ● PO Box 1
Thorndike ME 04986-0001 USA

(207) 568-3717

US & Canada:
1 800 929-9108
www.centerpointlargeprint.com